MADELYNNE ELLIS

More Titles to Love

The Black Halo Books
Come Undone
All Night Long
Off the Record
Come Together
All Fired Up
Come Alive
Reflex
Replay
Refrain
Revive
Reckless Beat
Rock Giant

Anything But...
Anything But Vanilla
Anything But Ordinary

Stirred Passions
Cherry Bomb
Black Velvet
Soul Kiss
Mint to Be
Screw Driver

Standalone titles
Tempted
You, Him, & Me
Don't Mess with my Relic
Sharing Adam
Gabriel's Naughty Game
Confessions of a Greedy Girl
Crazy Love

Gothic Urban Fantasy
Broken Angel Tale Possession: Three
Shapeshifting & Possession
Prophecy
The Demon Way
Shadow Queen

Scandalous Seductions
A Gentleman's Wager
Indiscretions
Phantasmagoria
Three Times the Scandal
The Viscount, His Lover & I
The Ghosts of Christmas Past
The Serpent's Kiss

Wooing the Wakefields
A Devilish Element

Romps & Rakehells
Capturing Cora
Seducing Sophia
Taming Taylor

Forbidden Loves
The Kissing Bough
Pure Folly

1

WYNTER

I'M GOING CRAZY locked up in this backwater.

Why the fuck did I ever imagine it'd be a great idea to record our second album here?

Oh, yeah, because it'd be quiet away from the city. No distractions. Out of sight of the tabloids. No record company execs breathing down our necks. Just the three of us. A state-of-the-art studio and the sea.

It'd be great, if we had the material we need to do the actual recording part. Sadly, the creative well is dry.

It's something they don't tell you when they get you to sign on the dotted line: the second is so much harder than the first. Common sense says it should be easier. After all, you've had practice. The thing is, while that first album involved a heck of a lot of blundering about, not knowing what we were doing, it was fuelled by dreams and the conviction that if we got it right, we'd make it.

Bravo. Well done. We did.

Second time around, there are things to live up to. Expectations that weren't there when no one knew who we were. Our first single was a smash. Our second and third both outsold it. The album's gone double platinum. Everyone's made a lot of cash. We should be enjoying it somewhere warm and full of people, instead... pebbles, and a pesky second album clause that might just be the death of us.

"We should check on Max," Reid says. He's lounging along the sea wall, the two of us having stepped outside for a quick breather forty minutes ago. Me, I can't see there's a desperate need to check up on our drummer. Reckon the worst that's happened to him is that he'll have scoffed all the scones and tanked himself up on Jolly's Cornish Ginger Beer.

Yes, I'm aware it's alcohol free, but I'm not sure Max has figured it out yet. He will eventually.

Reid's correct, though, we should get back to work, as watching the tide hasn't magicked any new lyrics into my brain.

His hand strays to my thigh. "Maybe if we..."

I don't pay any attention. Chances are his words are a repetition of one of the many suggestions we've already tried or vetoed.

Play in the dark.

Speed it up.

Slow it down.

Do it a cappella.

Inside.

Outside.

Upside down while swinging from the chandelier naked.

Okay, I vetoed the last one. Couldn't see how acrobatics and freezing my tackle off would create a spark of inspiration, and that's what I need. Inspiration. Something that gets the neurons firing. A catalyst. Fuck, I even tried blowing my best friend. Didn't give me the inspirational kick up the arse I need.

"Shit!" Said best friend, Reid, rolls off the wall landing on the shingle and starts scurrying towards the sea. I don't bother asking what's got him motivated, because now I'm pointed in that direction, I can see it too. There's a body... a person lying where the waves tickle the narrow band of sand. I hurdle the wall and crunch after him.

"Get Max," he yells.

I grab my phone out of my back pocket and call him. "Get down to the beach now! We found... person..." I've already forgotten about Max. "Is she breathing?"

Reid, on his knees in the shallows, presses his fingers to the pulse point in her neck and gives a juddery nod. She's a mess of tangled hair and clothing, with seaweed wrapped around her bleached limbs. "We need to get her inside."

"We need to check she's not injured."

"Tide's coming in."

And it does so with alarming speed in these parts. We've almost got caught out a couple of times.

"I can't see any obvious injuries."

By which he means there's no blood, or bones

poking out, though it's hard to be certain given the sullen sky and her bedraggled state. What the fuck happened to her? She's pretty, young, late teens, early twenties at a guess.

"How do we move her?"

I've a cartoonish image of us trying to lift her between us, an arm and a leg each. "We need Max." Luckily, bigfoot is currently skidding over the pebbles towards us. He arrives in a shower of them that half buries our girl.

"Sorry. Why haven't you moved her?"

I realise my phone is still connected, and so is his as our words are echoed back to us through our devices.

"We need a stretcher," Reid says.

"I can carry her." Max drops to one knee. I don't doubt that under normal circumstances he could, but she's soaked through, with the tide pulling at her, and the stony shore is almost impossible to walk on.

"Let's get her out of the water and then figure that out."

Turns out even that's not as easy as it ought to be. She's part buried in the sand and pebbles, with the weight of her clothing and the tide against us.

"'Pull, pull, me good lad. Pull, Winslow!'" Reid yells at us, which has the opposite effect, as both Max and I halt to scowl at him, while he continues scooping sand from around her like a dog hunting for bones. We watched *The Lighthouse*, a couple of nights back. What else do you view when holed up on a tiny island, besides watch a film about a couple of blokes stuck on a tiny island? Reid's been hunting the shoreline for mermaids ever since, and now the bugger's found one.

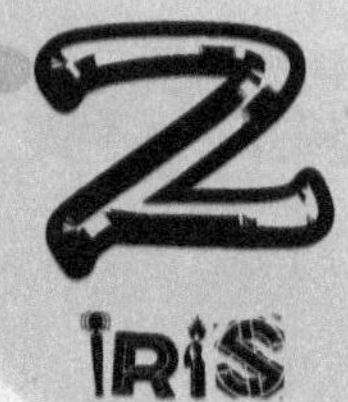

IRIS

WAKE NAKED in an unfamiliar room.

The sheets are clean, the décor, tasteful. Neither of those things tempers the panic that rises and threatens to pull me under much like the current that I remember all too vividly tugging me away from the shore.

Fuck! I'd been drowning. I was sure I was going to die. I guess if someone pulled me out, that explains the lack of clothing. You don't typically put people to bed dripping wet, but if I was found, why am I not in a hospital? Or at home?

I shiver at the thought of that place. A refuge I can rely on no more.

Cautiously, moving as slowly as I can so as not to make the bed creak and alert whoever lives here to my consciousness, I push myself upright against the pillows so I can get a better look at my surroundings.

It's not a lived-in room. Feels like an

upmarket B&B rather than someone's spare bed. There's a lack of personal artefacts, and everything is very pristine. Wallpaper, at a guess, is Laura Ashley, and there's not so much as a scuff mark on the skirtings.

I can see the door from here. There's a piece of paper taped to the back of it.

Taking the duvet with me, I cross to it and peel it free.

Hey, we saw this on the internet and thought you might appreciate it.

Don't panic. You're safe.

That does the precise opposite and spikes my anxiety enough that it becomes an effort to focus. It's okay being told not to panic, but that doesn't quell the rising tide of what the fuck do I do now that's simmering inside me, not helped by my dyslexia making the words see-saw and swirl.

Your clothes were wet, they're in the washer, but there's a set of clean things in the drawers. Sorry if they're a bit big. It's what we have.

If you need to use the bathroom, it's along the hall. First on the left. We don't have a spare toothbrush, but Max says you can have his. It's the blue one.

If you just want to leave, that's fine, but the tide might not be in your favour. Based on experience, it's always out when you want it to be in, and vice versa.

BTW you're on Liddell Island, if you know where that is.

We found you on the beach.

Okay, Reid found you on the beach. Pedantic bugger.

I read down the page, backtracking after each sentence to read it again, to make sure I'm interpreting it right. Liddell Island. It makes sense. The privately owned island is right across the bay. It's said a reclusive billionaire lives there, but it's also home to a posh restaurant, and allegedly, a recording studio. A causeway links it to the mainland at low tide, and at least one of the beaches has public access, which means I can cross without drawing attention to get home again.

Assuming I want to go home again.

I sit heavily on the foot of the bed and gnaw on my broken thumbnail.

It's not safe to go back there, but I'm without the resources to go anywhere else. If I go there, he'll be waiting for me.

If you had a purse, you've obviously lost it, so there's some money in the drawer with the clothes. It's not much. We had a whip round. Who uses cash anymore?

I can almost sense the shrug that accompanies that line. I wrench open the drawer and find a couple of notes and a handful of change, maybe thirty quid in total. It might get me to the next town over on the bus, but it won't get me a bed for the night. The clothing consists of a T-shirt, a pair of men's low waist skinny jeans, a pair of navy boxer briefs, and socks for someone with enormous feet. I pull them and the shorts on as I continue to read.

If you'd like some breakfast, kitchen is downstairs, then do a 180. Help yourself if we're not about.

If you want to say hello, and we're not downstairs, we'll be across the way in the studio. Go outside, and it's the barn-like structure on the left. Don't worry about disturbing us.

You won't be disturbing us.

Please disturb us.

Just not in a disturbing way. You've already given us a big enough fright.

Your not at all scary rescuers,

Wynter, Reid, & Max

Wait what? I yelp and drop the paper, only to pick it up and read the last line again with my mouth hanging open.

Wynter, Reid, and Max.

I read it again, and again... and again. It doesn't seem possible. Someone's obviously having a joke at my expense. I have not been pulled out of the ocean by the members of my favourite band. That's ridiculous.

This must be Harrison's idea of a joke. Sick bastard.

Doesn't explain where I am, though.

Maybe his mate's place. What's he called?

Lewis. I think his gran owns a B&B. Never would have thought it was as high end as this mind.

I'm being a fool. There's a window. All I need to do is look outside.

I scramble over the bed to do just that. Woodland and a steep bank. The property is detached, though. No immediate neighbours. Maybe I am where the letter claims? Maybe I'm not about to find Harrison on the other side of that door and won't have to endure his sick insinuations and threats.

My stomach rumbles as I pull the rest of the clothing on. It smells freshly laundered, but a faint lingering scent of something masculine clings to the fibres.

I hope my high-tops made it to the washing machine too, and I'm not trapped here barefoot. Socks are no substitute for shoes.

The moment I venture out onto the landing, it's apparent I am on Liddell Island. This is clearly a barn conversion, all exposed wooden beams and glass frontage through which I can see down to the pebbled shore, and way, way out across the bay, the town I've come from. I'm standing on a balcony overlooking the main living space, which is currently unoccupied, and the whole place smells of wood and sea air.

There's a laptop and the remains of someone's breakfast on the coffee table. A dogeared notebook, lying open, face down on the rug, as if someone hurled it towards the fire but missed. I pick it up. It's full of scribbled poetry and elaborate doodles. Flicking through it makes my throat turn dry. I'm not sure if I feel more like

Snow White in the seven dwarves' cottage or Goldilocks about to be scared witless by the three bears.

I find both porridge and apples in the kitchen. The world is fucking with me.

There's plenty of food, and the washing machine is still partway through the cycle. If I want to reclaim my clothes, I'm going to need to stick around. Thankfully, my footwear is in there too. Might as well at least have a drink. I click the kettle on and search through the nearby cupboard. It yields the required mug and an array of teas, plus coffee bags. I'd have been content with instant.

"Hey. You're up."

I jump. Astonished I've been so easily crept up on. Liquid goes everywhere. "Shitting hell!" Somehow, I manage to avoid scalding myself or soaking the borrowed shirt.

I turn to find a hulking brute of a man five inches from me, wielding a tea towel that he attempts to dry me with, while I attempt to back up.

I raise my hands in the universal sign of surrender.

3
IRIS

ET HER BE, Max."

A second man rests against the nearby cupboards, all laconic ease. He arches a ski-slope brow, evidently bemused by the interplay between me and the giant. Mister Laconic needs no introduction—Wynter Knight. A man I've harboured more than a few fantasies about.

I do indeed appear to be standing in Lucidity's kitchen.

Oh, and yeah, Wynter Knight is his real name. I'm sure his parents thought it was clever.

I gawp. This is crazy. I bashed my head. This is probably a hallucination. I'll wake in a moment, in hospital or still in the freezing water.

Fantasy land lingers on, despite repeated blinking. Wynter observes me, somewhat bemused. At least, I think that's what I'm seeing. Everything about Lucidity's singer-songwriter is so sharp that it gives him a malevolent edge. Chin, cheekbones, yes, even the slopes of his brows. Then there's his eyes. Green like poison.

He's hot for all that. Mind-numbingly so, in a way that makes me forget to breathe.

It's probably a good thing when the sandy haired behemoth blocks the view. I inhale deeply. He offers up a sheepish grin. It makes him look as if he's contemplating eating me but is trying to be polite about it. He towers over me, casting a shadow. I snatch the tea towel from him as if it might provide protection.

"I'm Max."

Yes, yes, he is. In every sense.

"Max Eden."

Lucidity's drummer. My knees quake. Reading his vital statistics online isn't the same as experiencing them in real life.

"And you're?"

"Iris," I gulp after the prompt. "I'm...I'm Iris." I set aside the tea towel and thrust out a hand.

Max grins. He forgoes my handshake. Instead, his two tree-trunk arms wrap around me and crush me to his solid chest. "You're okay now. I'm so glad you're okay, Iris." He pats my back as he squeezes.

This is surreal. The world has surely tipped on its axis. Max holds on, keeping me trapped between the cupboards and the solid wall of muscle that is his person, squashing the air out of me. But you know what? He smells good. A little spicy, a little citrus, undercut with his own signature musk. Is this the time to be thinking such things? I'm almost out of oxygen. And oh, hello, there's something maxi-sized hitting me in the hip.

"She might need to breathe, Max." A third man says. The last of the trio.

"Shut up, Reid, I'm counting."

Only instead of counting, Max mutters the lyrics to *November Rain*, that old Guns and Roses song my dad liked. Okay, I like it too, it helps me remember him.

"All done," Max says, releasing me at the end of the first verse. "Longer hugs are better for bonding. We all need to hug for longer. It's a fact."

"Right," I croak. I'm awash with something. Not sure if it's endorphins or terror. I gulp down air as I take a sly look at the area below his waistband and confirm what I already know. There's quite a package there.

"It's bollocks," Wynter remarks.

"It's scientifically proven, Wynt."

"It can be both those things at once," Reid diplomatically contributes.

Now that Max has released his grip, I can see around him to get a look at the band's lead guitarist. Reid Rushmore is wearing sweatpants that have holes in the knees, two odd socks, and a raglan shirt with grass stains up the sleeves, and wet patches across the front as if he'd recently gulped a bottle of water and mostly missed his mouth.

"All right, Ariel," he says. His grin is wide and utterly endearing, his hair a tangle of unruly brown strands inclined towards ringlets at the ends.

"Um, it's Iris."

"Don't bother," Wynter remarks. "He's convinced you're his personal Little Mermaid. Max, brunch for our guest, yeah."

"Right." The giant vacates his position looming over me and starts rummaging through the fridge.

"Any requests? Or you'll be getting the full works."

"Toast will be fine."

"Ah, now you're insulting him. Full works, Max. Why don't you bring your brew into the lounge, Iris, and give the man space to do his thing, and maybe you can tell us how you wound up here."

I'm not sure I have a definite answer. I can only surmise what happened after I hit the water. Nor am I sure I want to revisit the part that led to me jumping from the pier. My reluctance to part ways with the cupboards keeps me still, but it's soon obvious that Max needs the stretch of countertop to deliver whatever culinary masterpiece he's set on creating. The kitchen isn't large.

"Got a spot right here for you, Ariel," Reid calls.

Nervously, I follow Wynter back into the open plan living area.

"Reid," he snaps at his band mate, prompting Lucidity's lead guitarist to compact himself, ensuring there's room for me to sit. I do so warily, bottom perched on the edge of the leather, the remains of my brew still clutched tight in both hands.

"Thank you," I say, when neither of them

speak. "I'll get out of your hair as soon as my stuff dries."

"No rush. It's not like we're busy, or anything," Wynter remarks, a thread of sarcasm lacing his words, so that I'm not sure if he's narked about the interruption I've caused or not. Guess he has a sharp tongue to go with all those impressive edges. In contrast, Reid, the man beside me on the sofa, is like an oversized golden retriever. Scratch that, he's nothing so pedigree. He looks as if he's been dressed by a toddler and ate his last meal with one too, but warmth exudes from him like pheromones. He idly scratches an armpit, then widens the hole in the knee of his joggers.

"I appreciate the clothes and stuff." And them rescuing me.

"It's fine," Wynter says.

Reid flashes me a grin. "It livened up the evening no end."

I'll bet.

"Provided all sorts of inspiration."

"Lyrics?" Wynter quirks one of those evil villain brows.

Reid laughs.

"Fucker! Don't you fucking dare assault my eardrums with your fishy fantasies."

"Huh?" I contribute.

"Well, Ariel," Reid claps his hands and rubs his palms together.

"Someone set the table," Max hollers from the kitchen, cutting off whatever explanation Reid was about to give. Judging by his impish grin and the way he's unsubtly checking me out, that's maybe a good thing. I've a feeling whatever inspiration I provided in my comatose form may have leaned towards the sordid. After all, at least one of them got me naked. Was it Reid Rushmore, giant Max, or mister sharp edges?

The guys set about doing as Max asked. I sit back, after they wave away my attempt to help, and watch them work. They dance around one another in a well-practised rhythm. I still feel out of phase with reality. How can this be real? Last night was a nightmare, and now I've woken in heaven. Maybe that's it. Maybe I actually drowned. I give myself a sly pinch and instantly regret it. I have bruises that, in several places, such as my right thigh, have turned my skin into an abstract canvas of mottled blues and purples. If this was the afterlife, I'm sure I wouldn't feel so sore.

"Grub's up." Max arrives carrying all four breakfast plates at once. It's a fry-up. The sort of breakfast my dad used to make. Full of things that are bad for you but taste like heaven. I realise as the scent of eggs and bacon wafts up off the plate exactly how ravenous I am, and how desperate to tuck in. I skipped a meal last night, and lord knows where my next one will come from.

Max pulls out a chair for me and pushes it in once I'm seated. The guys ply me with both orange juice and a fresh brew, but despite the fact they obviously have questions, they don't press me while I eat. Only after I've set my cutlery down and pushed away my plate with a contented sigh do they give in to their curiosity.

"How'd you end up in the water, Iris?" It's

gentle giant Max who asks, and after the feast he's just served, I'm favourably inclined towards him.

"I jumped off the pier."

"Jumped jumped?" Wynter asks. "Or like jumped for a dare?" He exchanges concerned looks with Reid, whose brow furrows as he returns the gaze. I swear a whole silent conversation occurs between them.

"There was a guy following me," I admit, mostly because I don't want him to think that I'm suicidal.

"You fucking what?" Wynter growls. Apparently aloofness and sharp edges don't restrict his sense of moral outrage.

"A guy you know?" Reid's hazel eyes are riddled with curiosity.

I almost shake my head, before I cave and give a nod. Why pretend. "My stepbrother. He was waiting for me when I left work. Said he was there to make sure I got home safely." But the only danger was the one he posed. "I told him I could get home fine alone. He made a point of stalking off." I should have known better. He hadn't gone far.

"Do you live with him?"

I wobble my head from side to side. "Sort of. He was at uni, but he's recently come home. I live with his mum. Her and my dad married shortly before he passed away. It was okay, just the two of us, until Harrison came home. He's fine when she's there, but she's hardly ever home." Happens that she also thinks the sun shines out of her darling boy's arse. How can someone be so blind to a person's faults? Harrison is a misogynistic arsehole, who's been on my case ever since I first turned him down, which was precisely thirty seconds after he introduced himself as my stepbrother.

"So, you've nowhere to go?" Max says.

"I've been saving towards getting myself a place." I'm a way off having enough. I wonder what happened to my phone, my things. The bag with the novel I'd half-read. My bank card. Hell, even my house keys. Then again, maybe they don't matter, as I'm not setting foot there again, not even to collect my stuff, not when there's even a faint possibility of *him* being there.

"Do we need to call the police?" Wynter asks. "We didn't when we found you because..."

He doesn't impart a reason, and nor do the others. Doesn't take much fathoming out. If they had, it'd now be front page news that they'd found me, and I'm guessing they'd rather not have their whereabouts advertised.

"We will, obviously, if you want," Wynter says, his delicious voice full of hesitancy.

I shake my head. "No one saw anything. It'd be my word against his, and he'll say that I jumped of my own accord, and that he tried, but couldn't stop me." It'll even be the truth, of sorts. "You guys have been really kind, but I don't want to make things difficult for you. Seriously, you don't need to worry about me. Once my stuff is dry, I'll get out of your way."

"And go where?" Reid asks, there's something shrewd about the way he looks at me, that convinces me there's a sound mind lurking beneath his shambolic appearance.

Fact is, I don't have an answer. Tears well, but I avoid their gazes, so they don't see them.

"That's what I figured. You'll stay here until you work it out."

"What?"

My surprise is echoed by Wynter. "Reid, what the fuck? You can't just make that decision for us. No offence, Iris, but we don't know a fucking thing about her. She could be anyone, and in case you've forgotten, our position is precarious. We don't have time for this shit."

"I'm making time." Reid stretches an arm across the table to claim my hand.

"Me too," Max rises. He's tall enough that he casts a shadow. Wynter fails to quake in his boots. His sharp features transform into a scowl. "Guys!"

"What harm's she going to do? She's a little itty-bitty thing," Max insists.

"She could steal...."

"We'd have to have something worth nicking for that." Reid walks around the table. He puts his hands on my shoulders. "A little empathy, huh, Wynt. We fished her out of the fucking ocean eight hours ago. She's obviously been through hell. She's not got a phone or anything and has a cunt for a stepbrother. In comparison, our problems are a joke."

Wynter grumbles. "We need to focus."

Max starts stacking plates.

They're obviously here working, and I know nothing about the music business, but I know that studio time doesn't come cheap.

"Sure, and I'll do that better knowing she's here and safe than out there friendless, homeless, and fucking penniless. She stays." Reid kisses the top of my head, only to recoil. "Ariel, my sweet, you need a shower. Eau du seaweed is unbecoming on you."

4

MAX

IRIS BARELY REACHES the mezzanine level before Wynt and Reid start on one another.

"I know what you want, Reid Rushmore. This isn't about her or any kind of empathy, you want into her fucking knickers. That's it. You've seen her tits, and now you want a taste of them."

"Says the man who relieved her of her panties."

"She was fucking wet and comatose. And you removed her bra."

"Guys." I try, but they're not listening. There's no reasoning with them when they're like this. "Load the fucking dishwasher."

Miraculously, that part gets through and they dutifully tromp off to the kitchen. The squabbling doesn't let up. It's been this way ever since the jackass the label sent to produce our long-awaited second album made a mockery of it. Ever since, Wynt's been floundering. He insisted we ditch all that material and start over fresh. Problem is, there's not been a whole lot of fresh material flowing from his fingertips, and what little has, he ditches almost immediately as not being good enough.

The last time Reid tried to get him to see reason, they wound up taking swings at one another.

I hope they're not about to come to blows over Iris.

Maybe I oughtn't to have sent them to the kitchen, where there's crockery they could break.

Reid is obviously into her. Wynt too, or he wouldn't be so concerned about her being a distraction. I liked the feel of her in my arms. She's dainty, but she fit against me perfectly. Wouldn't mind enjoying a few repeats, maybe even some involving skin on skin. I'm going to check she has everything she needs.

I knock on the bathroom door. Iris opens it a crack. The shower is already running, and she has a towel clutched around her in a way that leaves her shoulders bare. "Oh," I say. "I brought you some clean ones. Wouldn't want to vouch for the ones in there."

"Thanks, Max." She offers up a sheepish grin and stretches an arm out to take them. Only the movement causes the tuck in her current covering to loosen. She squeals in alarm; drops the towels I just passed and clutches at the slipping fabric. I'm treated to a millisecond view of her luscious tits, before she hitches the bath sheet up an inch. The sides of it are swinging loose now, meaning her backside is bare, not that it's visible to me.

Still, the knowledge of its nakedness weevils its way into my head.

I bend to retrieve the towels from the floor. "Here."

Her cheeks are rosy when I stand, and I can't help but notice her gaze avoids my eyes and lands lower down. Her blush intensifies, when she realises my fly is being tested to its limits, thanks to the semi I'm now sporting. Beautiful woman, nipple flashes, and a naked arse, what do you expect? I'm only human.

"Hm, maybe... could you put them there?" She takes a couple of backward steps, allowing the door to swing inwards, and nods towards the heated towel rack. "Kinda have my hands full."

I step into the bathroom and do as she asks. "This stuff here is mine." I point out the bottles. "Feel free to use any of it. The three in one wash is Reid's. Wynt's is all the stuff in black bottles."

"Thank you."

I about turn to leave, and whoa... The mirror is right there behind her, giving me a perfect view of her peach-like arse. Dang, those bruises are ugly. They must hurt. I make a mental note to hunt out some arnica. Still, even marred by the bruises, my cock delights at the vision, and I sigh in appreciation. I've always been a bottom man. Big or small.

Oops! Iris's eyes widen as realisation strikes. "The mirror's... It's behind me, right?"

"Yeah." I admit, nose wrinkling as I offer up a sheepish grin. A cute full body blush sweeps through her skin.

"I'd like to shower now, Max... Max! Stop looking."

"But..." Might have slipped into fantasy land for a second there. "Right, of course. I'll leave you to it."

She follows me to the door, ready to lock me out. From downstairs something suspiciously like the sound of a plate smashing reaches us, followed by lot of shouting.

Worry creases Iris's lovely face. "Shit! Am I the cause of that?" She troubles her luscious lower lip. "I don't want to cause tension."

She's sweet, and they're being idiots. A door slams and then slams again. Seems they've taken it outside. "It's fine. They'll work it out." Hopefully. "I'll check on them. It's probably nothing to do with you. We're chasing a deadline. Everyone's stressed." I'm not sure she believes me.

"Thanks for the towels, Max."

"Not a problem. Anything, just ask. Especially if you need another hug. I've an infinite supply."

"Later, maybe." Her cheeks flame again. "Thank you for being so kind."

I shrug. "I do my best."

She closes the door, and I hear the bolt slide. Suppose I'd better go mediate between the guys, though by the time I get to them, they appear to have reached a standoff. They're sitting in their favoured spot on the sea wall, but turned away from one another, presenting equally stubborn visages.

"If this is about Iris, then she obviously can't

leave. She has nowhere to go, she's lost all her stuff, and her stepbrother is a threat."

"That's what I said." Reid turns his head to scowl at Wynt's back. "But muttonhead here won't see reason."

I take a perch to the front of Wynter. "You're seriously advocating that we send her packing?"

"We've enough to worry about without adding complications. I'd appreciate some acknowledgement of that fact. Plus, we don't know her from Adam, or that anything she's said is true. She could be anyone. Remember that girl in Vegas?"

If he means Cotton Candy, then we all remember her. She snuck her way into our dressing room, and hotel suites on a regular basis. "That woman was nuts. Iris is nothing like that. Also, dude! Our problems aren't nearly on the same scale as hers. We have homes to go and cash in the bank. And it's not like she sneaked her way in. We literally pulled her out of the sea."

Wynt sighs. "Yeah. It's just... guys, we have days left and fuck all to show anyone. I think our focus ought to be on the music, not some lass that washed up at our door."

"Maybe she's the inspiration we need," I propose.

Reid nods in agreement. "I find her very inspiring."

Wynter throws him an over-the-shoulder glare. "She might not be interested in banging you."

Reid laughs at the very notion. It is true that he attracts women of all ages in ways that defy logic. He's crass, ill groomed, more often than not dresses like he's an extra in a post-apocalyptic drama show, but that never seems to put them off.

"What can I say, I'm just it, man." Reid pushes his tongue firmly into his cheek. "You're just jealous."

"Of you? Fuck off."

"You're both awesome, obviously," I interject, mostly to stop the bickering, although they are both genuinely sound guys.

"I'm awesome-er."

I clip Reid around the back of the head for his refusal to let this die. It isn't new tension. Wynt believes he should get most of the attention owing to him being our frontman, and he does get a lot of it. The thing is, Wynt is standoffish, whereas Reid's a loveable rogue, and hence fans and interviewers gravitate to him.

"You're just worried she might be more into getting some of this," Reid says, as he runs his hands down his sides, "than what you're offering." He pouts and bats his eyelashes. "What's up, mate, worried the old Wynter charm's as defunct as your imagination, and that she'd rather ride me instead?"

"Fuck off."

"Reckon Max is in with more of a shot than you are."

Dunno why I'm always the consolation prize. "I like her, and I just saw her arse," I say, "but I don't think we should be talking about her in this way."

"Thank you," Wynt declares as if I've just backed up his point.

"I just meant, it's not for us to decide who she likes best."

"Why did you see her arse?" Reid asks, ignoring what I've just said.

"She was standing in front of the mirror; I got a glimpse."

"Fucker," Reid gripes, good-naturedly. "Were you there making your bid?" He punches my shoulder.

"Providing towels. She has some awful bruises. You should loan her your cream."

Reid isn't listening. "So, that's a yes, then." He gives an elaborate sigh. "Looks as if you won round one. Cooked her breakfast and provided fresh towels. She's totally gonna fall for you."

"I don't think—"

"I'm going for a walk," Wynt snaps. He slopes off, hands in his pockets, so his hipster jeans are at risk of sliding south.

"Great. What are we supposed to fucking do in the meantime?" Reid calls after him. "All you do is harp on about us working, but you're forever taking a breather. Why can't we just get in the studio and jam?"

"Don't," I say. "Yelling at him isn't going to help."

"Nothing fucking helps." He sighs and shakes his shaggy head of hair. "I don't care what he thinks, Iris is staying. You and me agree, and that's a majority vote, so Captain Misery can go swivel."

5

IRIS

AFTER A LONG, glorious shower, during which I'll admit I tried out each of the guy's products, I lie on the bed in the guest room. My clothes are still drying, so I start pulling the borrowed ones back on. I kid myself that I can tell what belongs to whom now that I'm familiar with their scents. I'm pretty sure the T-shirt belongs to Max, the skinny jeans are surely Wynter's, which means I'm wearing Reid Rushmore next to my skin. I run a hand over my hip where the soft cotton rests. It feels deliciously naughty, wearing someone else's things. I've heard of women borrowing their boyfriend's boxer briefs before, but it's not something I've ever done. I've certainly never entertained the idea I'd be this intimately acquainted with my favourite guitarist's underwear. Unsurprisingly, thinking about his smalls turns my mind to what they usually contain. It's not like I haven't had fantasies about these guys before. You know the kind, rockstar meets small town girl and falls madly in lust with her. Whisks her away from her fuck awful life to a new and exciting one. Their relationship is tested by hordes of non-believers, but they fall in mad passionate love anyway and proceed to have hot sex anywhere and everywhere, and orgasms are a daily guarantee.

Uh huh, yes please, I'd like some of that.

Except, is it Reid I want, or is it sultry, sexy Wynter? Then again, Max has turned out to be a surprising sweetheart. That cuddle was something else, and he's definitely been the one trying to make this the least weird for me. Also, he cooks. OMG, a man that cooks and doesn't just order takeaway when you're hungry. He's a keeper for definite.

Of course, I could be greedy. It is fantasy, after all. Just a girl, sitting on a bed with her own thoughts, wearing a guy's underwear, while touching herself. Why the heck can't I imagine having all three of them? One after another... or even all together.

I envisage a knock on the door, then three faces peering around the frame. Them smiling at me prone on the bed, hand inside my pants. Them entering, Reid losing his shirt as he strides towards me. He's inked beneath it. Wynter all cool but targeting my neck. Max a little bit awkward, leading with a hug, that he follows with a kiss, while Reid devotes his attention to my clit, and Wynter whispers all the things they're going to do to give me pleasure into my ear in that sexy, sexy accent of his.

I rub a little faster, still imagining Reid's going down on me.

A debate begins among them over who's going to fuck me.

"Guys," I reassure them. "It's okay, you can all have a turn." That thought makes me groan aloud. Wynter, Max, Reid... I picture each of them naked and erect. Each equally eager to give me what I crave.

"Reid," I say. "Reid, first."

"Damn right." Reid crawls up from between my legs to cover me. I get a glimpse of his handsome face before his lips meet mine and I groan all the need, all my desperation into his mouth. He's a sloppy kisser, all tongue and enthusiasm, but his body sits exactly right between my legs, and I want nothing but to rake my nails across his broad back and arch into him.

There's a knock on the door for real, and the hinges creak as it opens.

Startled, I jerk my hand away from my pussy, which leaves me reclining on my elbows facing the door in such a come and get me pose that it's no wonder Reid's eyebrows skyrocket when he sees me.

"Ariel," he says in a throaty drawl. I'm wearing his band mate's T-shirt and his now somewhat damp shorts. He looks at me expectantly, as if he's waiting for me to ask him something. "I heard you call."

"No. I—"

"You didn't call me? I distinctly heard you say Reid."

I shake my head. Did I say that aloud? Heat

fills my cheeks. What were the odds he'd be right outside my door and overhear me?

"Okay. If I'm not needed, then I'll leave you to..."

He grins.

Fuck, he knows. He knows what I was doing.

Then he shoots a finger at the jeans lying beside me. Right, he just meant he'd leave me to finish getting dressed.

He turns, but he does it slowly, which gives me a view of his very fine arse, and tells me he's lingering with intent, like he's waiting for an invitation.

"Stay," I squeak. "If you want... I mean, I could use some company."

He turns back immediately. "Almost forgot." He fishes a tube from his back pocket. "Max told me to give you this."

I take the offered cream and slather it over the worst of my bruises. Well, the ones that don't involve me exposing myself to Reid. He watches, fascinated.

"If you're staying, sit down. It's weird with you standing there gawping like that."

He shifts the jeans and sits beside me. "This must be really tough for you. I bet last night's playing havoc on your mind."

"Yeah, ish, trying not to dwell on it, to be honest." What I ought to be focused on is what I do next, not playing make-believe that I can command the attention of three guys at once.

"So, what are you thinking? Plans?"

I bow my head and give it a shake. "Not sure. I'm not... I can't go back there." I wonder what

Harrison has said to Cathy about my absence. Doubt he's told her I jumped into the sea to avoid whatever he had planned for me. Does he have regrets? Feel guilty? A flash of recollection pierces the void in my memory. Harrison leaning over the railings on the pier yelling obscenities. The water tugging at my clothes, dragging me away from the shore. Where I hit the water, it turned out to be much deeper and colder than I'd expected. I thought I'd be able to hide beneath the pier and wait until he left, then creep back up the shore.

"What can we—what can I do... to help?"

I shake my head. "You guys are busy, and I don't want... You need to focus on your music, not my shit. I've been waiting for your next single... album. I don't want to be responsible for holding it up."

"You won't be. Ignore what Wynter said. He's just tense. I'd rather you were here and safe than you left and..." He shakes his head, but there are protective vibes rolling off this man. I wouldn't mind hiding beneath his wing. "In any case, there ain't no music happening around here, just a truckload of moping. If magic was going to happen, it'd have done so already. You're the high point of what's been a miserable experience."

"That bad, huh?"

Reid flops backwards on the bed. "Pretty dire."

"How come?"

He rolls over so that he's facing me, and I mirror his pose. He seeks my hands and holds them in his between us. For a minute or so, his focus remains on our fingers, and it's clear he's chewing over what to tell me. I suppose it's natural that he'd be cautious. As Wynter pointed out, they don't know me, and given my financial situation, it's reasonable to assume I might sell them out.

"You guys totally blew up two years back, and then these last eighteen months, silence." They were slated to do great things. The music press loved them, but recently, there've been comparisons with other bands—The Stone Roses—that hit it big but never realised the potential their first offering predicted. Over the last few months there's been rumours that they'll split.

Reid flashes me a grin. "I guess you might call it a lack of confidence. You need music and lyrics to record a follow-up and the Wynter well is dry."

"Oh! How come? Did something happen?"

"Kinda. We got fucked over by a producer."

"I was going to guess relationship break up. I know my creativity tanks when I'm depressed."

"You're a musician?"

"Hell, no. I don't know one end of a guitar from the other. Photographer. Leastways, I'd like to be. It's the eventual plan, just isn't... It's kinda stalled at the minute." I've won awards, but that doesn't guarantee work, and I can't afford to set up on my own, not while I need to plough all my earnings into securing an alternate home for myself.

"Take some pictures of me."

"What? No." I wave him away.

"Seriously. Why not? You don't think some

sexy pics of my half naked body will net interest in you, or make you some cash?"

I think they probably would. What I say is, "You're not half naked."

Why did I say that?

Instantly, he's tugging his top off, revealing a toned torso, and yeah, some ink, but a lot less of it than I expected. What he does have are two very fine lines, forming a V, pointing down beneath the low-slung waist of his joggers. "Reid, I don't have a camera."

"Hm." He poses with one finger pressed across his full lips and the rest of his fingers splayed beneath his chin. "Not sure if I should run and get you one, or..." He holds that thought internally. "Make believe." He uses his thumb and forefinger to symbolise an imaginary camera. "How would you pose me?"

How would I pose Reid Rushmore? Exactly as he is right now, so at ease, so comfortable on my bed, half naked. The coppery light from outside painting the contours of his abs, and not a stitch of designer clothing in sight. "I'd just want you to be you."

"Come on, then. I'm not seeing any of these candid snaps being taken."

I try to bat him away again, but in the end, I play along with his wishes and take shot after shot with my imaginary camera. Close ups, and long shots. He sprawls on the bed. It's obvious he's had some experience of being photographed. Not a surprise, he's very photogenic.

"You know this island belongs to Alaric Liddell," he says, while I'm standing straddled across his body, taking fake downward looking shots.

"I've heard that, yeah."

"It's true. I could introduce you, if you like."

"Why would you do that?" Alaric Liddell is one of the world's top photographers. He had an exhibition at the Tate St Ives not so long ago that I visited repeatedly during its four-month run.

"Why wouldn't I?" He beckons me with a curled finger. "Come here, Little Mermaid." I kneel. Reid crunches into a sitting position, which leaves me straddled across his lap, him in his joggers and me in his boxer briefs. The combined heat of our bodies is tangible. "Hi," he says, eyes twinkling.

I bite my lip. "Hey."

He tilts his head. Blinks in a way that can only be described as flirtatious.

Fuck! Is he going to kiss me?

He nudges my nose with his nose.

He is.

Another nudge. I feel the whisper of his breath, then it's happening. Reid Rushmore is pressing my lips apart so that he can slide his tongue inside. And boy does he know what he's doing. Turns out my imagination got him all wrong. He's not the unskilled but enthusiastic amateur I supposed. No, he's a tease, a tormentor. He holds me in a grip that's equal parts deferential and possessive. His worship makes me groan. It heats me up, steals my breath away, then makes me come begging for more. I follow him backwards so that I'm sprawled over his half naked body, our hips perfectly aligned.

"I'm not sure this is a good idea." I mutter when we part for breath.

"Why's that?" His hands settle solid upon my hips, and he rocks me back and forth against him.

"I don't generally get off with guys I've known five minutes."

Harrison liked to call me names. Easy, sluttish... Worse... That's if he wasn't chastising me for being the opposite—frigid, repressed. He just didn't like the fact that I didn't like him. His ego couldn't handle it. I don't put any weight on his opinion, but still, those labels echo in my head as Reid's touch intensifies.

"It's been well over half a day since we met," he says.

"Practically a lifetime," I deadpan. "Does it count if I was comatose for most of it?"

"Give me one good reason why we shouldn't. If we're attracted to one another, and we're grown adults of sound mind, then what's the issue?"

I don't have one. He's right. There shouldn't be one. I should bask in my good fortune at discovering Reid Rushmore, a guy admired by millions is into me.

"Can't think of one, huh?" Reid purrs against my skin. He starts on my neck, kissing, and then sucking hard enough that I'm sure he's leaving marks. I can't quite bring myself to stop him. The body's willing, and my mind is only putting up a feeble show of resistance. Is this what I want to do? It is, right? Only, what happens once we're done? Do I then get ushered on my merry way?

Reid wriggles his way down my body. I barely realise he's doing it, until I realise his erection is no longer branding me as his tongue skims over my breasts, and paints circles around my nipples.

"I really want to taste you, Ariel." He kisses me midway down my abs and hooks a finger under the waistband of the briefs.

"It's Iris, and Reid..." My hands seek his shoulders, and he looks up at me with his pretty hazel eyes. That's almost enough to convince me to let him carry on. I would really like to feel his mouth on my pussy, but I take a breath and say, "Stop," instead.

He cocks his head, but doesn't resist when I shift, so that I'm no longer astride him.

"You okay?" he asks.

I nod, snatch up the forgotten jeans, and pull them on. "This is all just... It's a lot. I need to..." I make a lowering motion with both hands. He watches me while I bite my lip. "It's not that I don't want to. I just..."

"Your stepbrother fucked you up."

"Yes—no. It's a bit of that, but not really."

"So, what is it then?"

I cross my arms across my chest, uncertain myself. Maybe just the sheer fact that I feel so vulnerable in my borrowed clothes and motley of bruises. "We only just met, Reid, and colour me wary after everything that happened last night."

His pupils grow wide. "Did that fucker assault you? I thought the bruises were from the sea."

I shrug. "I didn't stick around long enough to give Harrison a chance to lay a finger on me. I took a dive instead." At the time it seemed the better option.

"Shit, I'm sorry. That fucking arsehole. If I meet him, I'm going to wring his neck."

His fury makes me smile.

"Thank you for stopping when I asked."

He nudges my arm, then pulls me into a hug.

"No, I'm sorry for not being considerate, and taking advantage when you're all vulnerable."

"You didn't."

"Did."

"And you stopped when I asked."

He frowns. "Only an absolute arsehole would do otherwise, and I hope I'm not that."

"I'm pretty sure you're not."

Okay. We both breathe sighs of relief.

"How about a walk?" he asks. "Might help us both cool off, and I could show you the island. We could go see if any of your stuff washed up."

Given he's still perky in a very particular place, that sounds like a good idea. Not that I think finding my missing bag will help. The book is going to be unreadable, and my phone bricked. I point to my feet. "Bit lacking in the shoe department." I'm feeling battered enough without risking a foot injury by striding about outdoors bare foot.

"Reckon there's a pair of flip-flops around, and we can go down to the beach."

The beach is only a very short walk away. Reid takes me over to where he found me last night. "About here." The tide is way out, revealing a vast stretch of orangey sand and forests of bladder wrack and sea spaghetti beyond a narrow band of pebbles. There's no sign of my bag.

"Bet I gave you a fright."

"Yeah."

In the distance we see a man with two dogs. "That's Ric. Let me catch up with him." He sprints off at a pace I can't hope to match, especially not in my borrowed footwear. Pretty soon, he vanishes from view. The sky turns grey not long after, and the wind picks up. Chilled, I turn back to the row of houses.

There are five buildings in total. Two or three have probably always been houses, the others are clearly converted barns or boathouses, or something like that. I recall the note from earlier said that the one now on my right is the studio.

Steps lead up from the beach to the sea wall. When I emerge onto the paved plaza that connects the buildings, I find Wynter sitting with his back to the seawall.

What's he doing here? I stroll over to him. "Hey."

He slowly looks up my body. "Iris."

"Wynter."

"Something you need?"

"Not sure." I sit beside him. "I'm sorry I caused a distraction. I didn't mean to derail whatever you guys are working on. I'm looking forward to your second album."

"Are you?" He groans, making it clear that wasn't really a question. "Well, Iris, I'm not sure there's going to be one. Leastways, not any time soon."

I'm not sure what to say to that that won't sound either trite or condescending. I'm sorry you feel that way, sounds both to my ears. "Maybe you just need a break."

He scoffs. "Wouldn't that be grand! Ain't happening. I'm stuck here and the clock's ticking. I've a handful of days to deliver a solution or we get ditched."

"Your label would really follow through on that?"

"We're costing them money. And we're not getting younger while we do it."

Unbelievable. "You're what, twenty-four?"

"Twenty-six."

"That's hardly ancient."

"We're not fresh anymore. We're not green kids who do as they're told because they're so star-struck and terrified of losing their one shot that they bend over backwards to please. We've seen how it works. We're yesterday's news. Washed up."

It's always said that the music business is ruthless, but hearing it first-hand makes it real. I hurt to my stomach for him... for all three of my rescuers.

"Reid says you're blocked, but I saw your notebook. It looked pretty full of ideas."

"Did it, indeed. Took a good look did you?"

I raise my hands. "No, I didn't read it. It was obviously private. I just saw it. It was on the floor. I picked it up."

He gives me a hard look with those livid green eyes, lips pursed. I lean back, anticipating a cobra-like strike, or at least a pithy remark, but I sustain neither wound.

"Most fans would have photographed it or stolen it outright."

"But then they'd miss out on those ideas

becoming something. Isn't there anything good in there?"

I'm sure there must be. The bits I saw seemed deep and meaningful.

He angles his head back so that he's gazing at the sky. "If you'd asked me four months back, I'd have said yes."

"So, what changed?"

Wynter shakes his head and brings his fingers to his mouth, where the digits play along his plump lower lip. After a minute or so, it becomes obvious I'm not going to get an answer.

"I'm a photographer. When I get stifled, I soak up other media. I listen to music, read, go places, just try to fill the creative well."

He nods, but it fast turns into a shake. "I'm not interested in listening to everyone else's finished masterpieces."

"So, a film. There must be something you want to watch that qualifies as pure escapism."

"There is one thing I've been putting off."

He names a recent blockbuster I wouldn't have expected him to like, starring Felicity Caine, a former child star that I used to love watching in the Caine Chronicles as a teen. Dad used to watch with me. We had a deal: he'd watch my choice, and I'd watch his. We'd both pretend it was a chore and that we hated the other's choice, but we never missed a single episode of either show. "Watch it."

"It's supposed to be my reward for finishing the album."

"Sometimes you have to cut yourself a break and just eat the chocolate."

He absorbs my advice with a frown.

Reid reappears. He towers over us, peering at us suspiciously. "Everything all right?" It's a reasonable question, given how Wynter and I are frowning at one another.

"Fine," I say.

Reid offers me a hand up. "I spoke to Ric, he said you can pop over tomorrow and see his setup, with the caveat that you subject yourself to his scrutiny. Apparently, everyone who enters his studio is fair game.

"Iris is a photographer," he explains to Wynter.

"Yeah, she said."

Not that I'm about to turn the offer down, but what will Alaric Liddell see when he analyses me through his viewfinder in my bruised and battered state? I'll endure it, no matter. Anything for the opportunity of a one-on-one meeting with him.

Life has certainly become interesting since my arrival on Liddell Island.

RIC'S INVITATION SETTLES the question of Iris's presence. After dinner I let her use my laptop so she can access her bank account, cancel her cards, and order new ones to be delivered here. Wynter remains silent regarding what that means in terms of her continued presence. He seems to have warmed to her a little after their chat earlier.

Plus, he has sisters, and I pointed out that he might want to think about how he'd like them to be treated if they ever found themselves in a similar situation.

I find him sitting in the dark in the lounge long after we've all said our goodnights and retired to our respective rooms. He's drinking whisky neat and striking matches one after another, letting them burn right down until the flames almost touch his fingertips before blowing them out.

I pad downstairs and take possession of the

matchbox. "We need those to light the fire." Something I do. It's chilly down here in the dead of night. The dry kindling catches, and the flames give the shadows an orange tint.

There's no point in asking what's up, I already know. I thread myself around him and wrap him in a hug. Initially, he resists, but I don't let up, and eventually he caves and sinks into my embrace.

"You need to let everything that knob-end said and did go." I brush my lips against his temple where the skin is thin over his skull.

"What he did hurt."

"I know." It hurt all of us, but those songs poured from Wynter's heart, making the attack far more personal. It's soured the whole creative process for him. Dammit, he never asked for someone to come in and fix his work. It didn't need fixing.

He pulls another match from behind his ear and strikes it against the grain of the side table. He lets it burn until it singes his fingertips. I blow it out before he gives himself some serious burns. "You need your fingers to play, remember? You should run your hand under the tap."

He doesn't budge, so I head to the kitchen to fetch a cup of icy water. It's something. When I return, Iris is perched on the sofa in the spot I recently vacated. She's wearing one of Max's oversized shirts. It skims her knees, leaving the lower part of her comely legs on display. Her knees are scraped, but otherwise the skin there is unmarred. She holds up the TV remote. I watch from the doorway as she starts scrolling through the Netflix offerings.

She stops on the new Jack Bold film I know Wynter's been itching to see, but putting off, claiming he hasn't earned the right to view it yet. Silly bugger. He thinks he's dangling carrots to incentivise himself, really, he's torturing himself for being a failure.

Max leans over the banister from the mezzanine. "Are you guys having a watch party?"

The wooden stairs groan as he descends. I return to the kitchen and brew up four hot chocolates with marshmallows, squirty cream, and sprinkles. It's about the extent of my culinary ability. I carry them through on a tray.

"You forgot snacks," Max says, claiming a cup.

"I made drinks."

He flips onto his feet. He's an agile bugger for all that he's both tall and bulky. I settle on the left of Iris. When Max returns, he sits on the floor with his back against my knees.

We eat. We drink. And we watch.

No one speaks.

No one tries to lick the chocolate moustaches from anyone else's top lip, but it's comfortable and settled in a way that it hasn't been for far too long.

At the sixty-minute mark, there's a sex scene that requires the strategic locationing of some of the square sofa-parasites. Guess they have a nondecorative purpose after all. Iris hides her face behind hers. God she's cute.

Shortly after, she rests the cushion on my knee, and her head on it. Her legs wind up across Wynter's lap. He wrestles a throw off the back of the sofa and wraps it around her. I guess she trusts us, because within another ten minutes, she's asleep and making sweet little purr-like snores.

Wynter turns his head. "Is that her?"

"Yup," I nod.

He grins. Properly grins in a way that I've not seen in forever. It lights up his eyes and smooths all the harsh edges from his face. "Should we move her upstairs?"

When Max attempts to lift her, she stirs, rubbing her eyes like a sleepy animal in a Disney movie.

"Sorry, I think I dozed off." She glances at the screen, which is back to showing the viewing options. "Damn, guess I missed the end. Did the good guys win?"

"They did," Wynter says.

"It's okay, Max. I can walk myself up the stairs." She brushes off his attempt to lift her.

We all rise. I turn off the TV, while Wynter slides the guard across the fire.

"Too soon for a sleepover?" I ask her, as she heads for her door. Her room is next door to mine.

"Goodnight, Reid."

"Guessing that's a yes."

"You might not like me so much after you hear me snore."

Consummate gentleman that I am, I decline to inform her that all three of us have enjoyed that privilege.

7

IRIS

REID IS QUIET on the walk over to the fort Ric Liddell calls home. To our surprise, Wynter accompanies us. He hasn't said anything else about me leaving since the initial outburst. It seems the matter is settled. The pair of them drop me at the door. They don't even wait for the owner to answer before abandoning me in favour of studio time. I hope they don't resume arguing once I'm no longer standing between them.

The man who opens the door is older. Mid to late thirties at a guess. His blond hair hits his waist, and tattooed biceps peep from beneath both sleeves of his band T-shirt for a metal group of old. He's not what I expected, not that I had any definite expectations. Maybe a nondescript white guy in a turtleneck, or a deliberately quirky one, decked out in hippy motley. He's neither. He's hot. And clearly a metal fan. He'd make a good subject for one of his own photographic studies.

"Iris, I presume. Ric." He shakes my hand and leads me inside. "Studio's up top, so I hope you don't mind a climb. Reid says you washed up on my shore the night before last. Most visitors use the causeway."

"Sorry, yeah. I hope I'm not intruding." I'm already conscious of disrupting Lucidity's studio time, without adding wasting the time of my favourite role-model to my catalogue of disasters.

"You're not. You're saving me from paperwork. This afternoon was looking dire. Now I get to spend it doing what makes me happy instead." I didn't even realise that he had a camera in his hand until I'm the focus of his viewfinder. "Payment for the guided tour," he says.

My entrance into his tower-like abode is accompanied by barking from within.

"Don't worry, they're fastened in the kitchen."

A spiral staircase leads us up numerous levels to his attic studio. It occupies the entire top floor, and it is fashioned into different zones, including an obvious chill out zone and an editing suite, alongside a plethora of lights and stacked canvasses. There's none of his work displayed, which is disappointing. The walls are all pale neutral shades, except for one corner that's painted black. It's a fabulous space, and I spend a good twenty minutes pottering about, taking it all in, and flicking through the canvasses that are stacked facing the walls. Turns out that's how he stores them.

Most of his work is shot in black and white. All

of it is breathtaking. Ric blends into the background, so I'm only vaguely aware of him shooting me from every angle, while I ask mostly inane questions. Every now and then, I unwittingly stare straight into the camera lens, and I hear a click and a whir of digital camera, and he'll smile like he's gained something.

People used to think that being photographed somehow trapped a piece of your soul. I wonder if that's what prompts his smile. He's just claimed a piece of mine.

"What have you produced so far?"

I use his computer to show him my online portfolio. He views without comment, leaving me to interpret the nuances of his expression for potential interest. At least he doesn't tell me I'm rubbish and not to waste my time.

"I don't suppose you need an assistant, do you?"

My time here is surely nearly up, so, yeah, I'm asking. It'd be a wasted opportunity otherwise, and I don't want to live with that regret.

The blond vision before me laughs like I've said something utterly hilarious. "You offering?"

I nod. "I'd love—"

"Lady, you'd change your mind after five minutes. I'm what's kindly referred to as a high maintenance hermit, or an antisocial arsehole, when people aren't saying it to my face."

He agreed to this meeting; he can't be that much of either of those things.

"Worth the risk," I suggest. I really would love to learn from him. "I'd be here to absorb your genius as well as make myself useful."

"Flattery isn't going to cut it. Although, I can't say I don't sometimes fancy a dogsbody. It'd mean you living here on the island..."

"Sounds great." I need a new home.

He chuckles. "You say that, but... Maybe, I'll consider it." He does so for perhaps half a second before shaking his head. "Not worth the frustration for either of us."

I'm not as ready to let the idea go. "I work hard, and I'm good at blending in."

"I'm sure the first of those is true, the second..." He rocks his hand indicating the jury is out on that one. "What you are is a sweet young thing. What makes you so sure you can hack it? I know you've flicked through those." He gives the canvasses a nod. "But are you actually even familiar with my work?"

"I went to your exhibit at the Tate seven times, and I—"

He cuts me off. "Once it's printed on a canvas, people call it art, but while I'm making it, it's messy, it's crude. It's rude. It's one hundred per cent real, and hence, pornographic. People have sex in this studio while I photograph them."

"Yes, I realise."

"Do you? Ever watched two or more people get that intimate. Photographers—we're the ultimate voyeurs. For most people, what I do is way out of their comfort zone."

I recall last night's film, and how it made me squirm. Maybe Ric has a point. With experience, I'd get over that though, wouldn't I? It seems to me that the thing to do here is to be honest. "I won't lie and claim I wouldn't be embarrassed. I would, but I'd adapt, learn to distance myself. And art is sometimes discomforting. Don't I need to feel that, if I want to portray it?"

"Here..." He hands me a camera. A camera so expensive I'm instantly terrified I'm going to drop it. "I'll be honest, Iris. I'm not really interested in whatever you have to say. There are plenty who can talk the talk, but can you capture the essence? Look, Reid obviously likes you. I like Reid. That's why I let you in here, and it's why I'm giving you a chance to show me what you can do. I'm not looking for an assistant, but I try to do my bit to sponsor young creatives. Give me a reason to invest in you."

I clutch the camera, which now feels like a million-pound grenade. "What should I—"

He shakes his head. "Your vision, Iris. Not mine. Show me what you see. Show me what's in here and in here." He indicates both my heart and my head. "Let me see what makes Iris—"

"Allen," I provide.

"—Iris Allen, tick."

He snaps another candid shot of me. I expect I look like a kid who just met Santa for the first time.

"Happens I think I already know, but I could be wrong. You may yet surprise me."

I want to ask what he thinks that is, but I don't, and I'm ushered out.

My head's in the clouds as I head back to where Lucidity are staying. I can't believe I have this opportunity, but now the pressure is on not to waste it. I take a few landscape shots as I walk, but I already know that what I really want to do is photograph the guys. Please let Reid still be into the idea of posing for me. Although, I'm not so sure I want to capture anything so staged.

The polished poses that fill the media, while beautiful, aren't nearly as intriguing as the candid shots of them behind the scenes. Not to me, anyway. I think of the differences between the version of Reid the world sees, and the real man who dresses in odd socks and has more holes in his clothes than a sack infested with moths.

It's not just him, it's Max and Wynter too.

There are facets of them both that their fans don't get to see, but which I have the means of capturing. If they'll let me.

I really hope they'll let me.

Doubts hit me hard as I get closer to the studio complex. What's to say that in my absence, Wynter hasn't persuaded the other two that it's time I left?

I knock on the residence door, but no one answers, so I let myself in. No one's home, and though I want to, I'm too afraid of causing a distraction to brave infiltrating the studio and risk precipitating a drama.

Max is the first to reappear. After taking a few photos around their living space, and raiding the cupboard for snacks, I've been chilling with a book in my room. It's a spicy one, presumably left behind by a previous resident, where a group of old friends reunite and previous passions reignite.

I find Max in the kitchen.

"Iris," he greets me, while rifling through the fridge-freezer. "I'm thinking pizza and salad for lunch, unless you don't like that."

"I've heard of mythical beasts who don't like pizza, but I've never met one. Unless you're covering it in banana and pineapple, then I'll pass."

"No fruity pizza, duly noted." He starts piling ingredients onto the worktop, including three varieties of cheese, various forms of peppers, fresh spinach, and slices of pepperoni. Plus, a head of lettuce and olives... and more olives. Someone obviously likes them.

When he said pizza, I assumed he meant the pre-prepared kind you pull out of the freezer and throw in the oven, not that he was going to make it from scratch. He has fresh dough in a tea towel covered bowl.

"What did you think of Ric?"

"Intimidating."

"Not sexy? When we all met him, we were like, 'Fuck he's hot!' And loaded. How bloody unfair is that?"

"Hot in an intimidating way, maybe." There's no denying that Alaric Liddell is blessed in the looks department, but I've never been into the whole metal scene. I'm a pop punk girlie. "He's not really my thing."

"That true, Iris?"

I give a nod, and he seems pleased.

"He's loaned me a camera and told me to impress him. Not sure I have that in me, but it won't hurt to try."

Without blinking, he says, "Of course you can do it, Iris. You're gonna blow his socks off."

"Do you think he wears them?"

"Every time I've seen him, he's been in

stonking great boots. If he doesn't wear socks with them, he's officially weird."

"I think he was barefoot just now."

"And that's why you're gonna nail this. You see details." He extends an arm towards me. "Come here, let me give you a hug."

"What for?"

"Assurance? And because it's hug 'o clock."

"Is that an official time?" I glance at the digital clock display on the microwave expecting it to be spelling it out. It's a little after midday.

"Definitely."

Max swaddles me. Being held by him is like being wrapped in a weighted blanket—calming, reassuring. All the pressure points in my body sigh as they're stimulated.

"How are your bruises doing?"

"Yellowing. The cream helped."

He keeps the cuddle going.

"You give great hugs, Max."

"So do you." He kisses the top of my head, which prompts me to raise my chin to look up at him. Our gazes meet, and there's something... a connection.

He lowers his head and kisses my lips.

Oh, God. Oh, fuck. I don't want it to end, but I ought to stop him. I already kissed his band mate. Hell, I almost made it to third base with him. But damn, the tingles kissing this gentle hulk of a man creates are too big a thrill. He lifts me, and before I know it, I'm perched on the worktop, my legs wound around his hips and he's rubbing against me, driving the seam of my borrowed jeans right against my clit in a way that creates fires that even icy water couldn't put out.

"Max. I think you should know that I made out with Reid earlier."

"I know that, Iris. He told us."

He told them.

"It's okay. It's not a problem. We've all kissed the same girl before."

I'm not sure what to do with that information. "You have. Doesn't that cause—"

"We're good at sharing."

I believe that of Max. Can just about convince myself of Reid's generosity, but Wynter? He seems the possessive type, who probably won't even loan you a paperback, let alone contemplate allowing his bandmates to smooch a girl he was into. Not that he's into me, just maybe no longer hates me.

Do they really not mind, or am I now at the centre of some sort of competition?

"Can I touch you, Iris?"

That yanks my focus back to the here and now.

"Well… Um…" His mouth is on mine again as he reaches for my fly, and while I'm sure I should stop him, I'm equally certain I absolutely shouldn't. It's only a day on from my close encounter with Reid, and I think I'd like to explore that chemistry further.

"Why have you all shared… kissed the same woman before?"

Max gives me a goofy grin, like I've asked something with such an obvious answer he's flummoxed how to respond. "We all liked her."

"Right, but…"

"It was on tour. She was part of the crew, and there's not much time for external relationships when you're moving about that much, so as we all liked her, and she liked all of us, we figured something out. Happens there was some experimenting too. Got to be a few perks of being a rock star, right?"

"And it worked?"

"For as long as it needed to."

"But she didn't stick around?"

"This is a lot of questions, Iris."

"I'm just trying to understand."

"An opportunity came up with another band. She moved on."

"Were you sad?"

"A little."

"Reid and Wynter?"

"Never asked them. Iris, is this your way of saying no?"

Is it?

8

MAX

I EXPLORE HER mouth, and she explores me. There's something about our gorgeous houseguest that makes me come over all needy and protective. I want to make her world well again, and to help her realise her potential. Why? Well... Iris is adorable for one. Beautiful for another. And I've a feeling she's the missing piece we've been waiting for to make Lucidity whole again. It's a gut feeling, a certainty that she washed up at our door for a reason.

Maybe the fix is as simple as the way she makes me feel like a flesh-and-blood person, rather than a caricature of a man. The three of us, we've all been walking around like empty shells for months, drained of all the vitality we once had in abundance, our creativity stifled by expectations, or ruined by charlatans who ought never to be allowed near a sound studio. A fucking producer should know better than to overload things with so many layers. Nothing had any room left to breathe. Even the drums got smothered. Complicated doesn't always equal genius. It's like cooking. Sometimes the best meals are the simplest.

Iris's hands tighten around my biceps as she clings to me. She's uncomplicated, unlike Wynter. I like her for that. There aren't layers you have to peel away to figure out what she's thinking.

She wears her heart on her sleeve.

Kissing her is like supping on nectar.

Sweet. Pure. And addictive.

Then, when I rub against her, the purrs in her throat make my cock stiffen to the point of discomfort, trapped as it is behind the rigidity of my zip. If she'd only slide a hand downwards, relieve the pressure.

I need more friction. Crave the touch of her hand and the velvet heat of her pussy.

It takes a bit of manipulation, but I free her of the tangle of borrowed clothing, then I capture her gaze and wet two fingers while she's watching.

The look in her eyes as I lower them is intoxicating. Surprise. Desire.

"Max," she groans as I tease said digits along the split of her pussy, then pinpoint my focus on her clit.

She's wet and hard as a pearl.

"Oh, God!"

She jerks against my touch, rocking her hips to meet the strokes. It all becomes instinctive between us.

I lick a line up the side of her throat. "Unfasten my fly, baby."

That is all the encouragement she needs. Air

kisses my skin, then her hand encompasses me. We stroke one another, heads pressed together, breathing in one another's excited gasps.

"Am I easy for doing this?"

"Am I?" I counter.

She immediately shakes her head.

"Then nor are you."

"Even though I made out with Reid?"

"Even if you do so again."

Her face lights up like I've said something magical. Like she was looking for raindrops and found diamonds instead. "I really want to fuck you," I say. I want her to know how much I want her. "But I don't want to rush you, if you're not..."

She applies her hungry mouth to mine, and her dainty hands rake across my back. "I want you, Max."

"We'll take it slow."

"We don't have to."

We do. I'm a big guy, and she's titchy, besides, I want to watch her come, and once I'm inside of her, I'll be too far gone to truly appreciate the beauty of it when she comes apart.

"Max," she gasps again, encouragingly. It's a sound I want to hear again and again. This is crazy, but good crazy. Sometimes you have to let go, say shove it to the rules, and just follow your instincts. It doesn't matter if she's into my band mates too. I still want this. I still want her.

I get my thumb in on the action, using it on the underside of her clit while I use my fingers to give her a taste of what's to come. Hardly takes a moment before she's groaning out her orgasm and flooding my hand with her juices.

"Fuck," she cries. "Fuck... oh, fuck." She tries to reel me in, as her muscles spasm around my fingers.

"Put it in, Max."

"So needy," I tease. "You can have a little taste, but no more than that until after dinner."

"I don't want to wait until after dinner. More now, please. Max!"

I obligingly give an inch. It takes every bit of my strength not to push deeper. None of this was planned. I didn't come prepared, and I don't carry condoms around in my pockets.

"I'm on birth control," she ventures. "If that's what's holding you back."

Shivers race through my body. The grip of her is intoxicating. I'm only just inside her. It doesn't count as penetration. Not really. "Don't tempt me."

I'll succumb if she does. I know I will. She's like my personal Siren. At her command, I'll obey her every wish. It'd be so easy to pull her forward right onto me.

She wriggles and gasps as I stroke the head of my cock through her wetness away from her entrance and up to stroke her clit. The way she gasps reminds me of the shiver of my high-hat when it's tapped extra lightly.

"I never thought you'd be into torture."

"This is agony for me, too."

I watch her as I tease my cock back and forth between where she wants me to slide and the external pleasure point that's now hard as a bead.

She wails as I touch her there. Makes a frantic

grab for the nearby tea towel and shoves it into her mouth.

The late afternoon light streams through the window over the sink to our left, and paints licks of amber through her hair. She spits out the towel to lock our lips again, while her fingers press into the small of my back, coaxing me closer.

I could do it. So rarely am I ever first at anything. I'm only a narrow thread away from casting caution to the wind.

Last of us to ever be kissed. Last to know the divine sensation of wet pussy cradling my cock. Last to discover my musical ability.

I'm the afterthought. The other guy in Lucidity.

Iris never makes me feel like that.

"Hey, how long is food going to be?"

Wynter makes an abrupt halt just over the kitchen threshold.

Iris's cheeks flame. She turns her head as if removing Wynt from her peripheral vision will excise him from reality.

"Got a little sidetracked with our guest."

"Yeah. I can see that."

He about turns and exits to the lounge.

Tears tumble down Iris's cheeks. "He's gonna tell Reid."

I was going to tell Reid.

"Iris, I told you. You don't need to worry. This isn't going to cause issues." I'm not sure how to convince her of that.

Wynter returns. "Figured you might need one of these." He slaps a condom foil down on the countertop beside us but accidentally catches the coffee spoon as he does. It flips up, and lands on the floor. Automatically, he retrieves it. He can't reach the sink to drop it there.

The longer he lingers, the more certain I become that I'm not going to need it. I can feel Iris tensing. He's gawping at us. Well, at her. At her splayed thighs and the ruby lips of her pussy.

"Wynt, some space, eh?"

"Sure." He slides out of the room, this time closing the door behind him.

I press our brows together. Iris giggles, her nerves getting the better of her. It makes me do the same. The tension dissolves a little.

I nudge against her, run my nose over her cheek as I seek out her lips again.

"Still want this?"

She answers by wrapping her arms around my neck and exploring my mouth with her tongue. "Fuck me and then feed me," she whispers into my ear as I roll the protection on.

"Cute."

I sink into her and it's as heavenly as I predicted. Our bodies mould perfectly. She's barely a weight in my arms as I make her sweat and groan.

When I come—far faster than I'd like. I want it to last forever—it's with the combined scent of Wynt's shampoo, Reid's aftershave, Iris's skin, and the nearby washing up liquid in my nostrils.

9

IRIS

I EAT, CONSCIOUS that I'm starving again, but I barely taste a bite. Max's efforts are wasted on me. I'm so nervous of what the other two members of Lucidity will say about me hooking up with Max that I don't even have the nerve to ask them if they're willing to be the subjects of my efforts to impress Ric.

Afterwards, while Wynter and Reid clear the table and load the dishwasher, Max coaxes me onto the couch. "You need to stop beating yourself up. You haven't done anything wrong, Iris. We haven't done anything wrong."

It's clear that he believes that, but it's much harder to convince myself, especially when part of me would love to believe I can have them all. Yes, even frosty, Wynter. He's thawing, and I keep getting glimpses of what's beneath, and it's obviously a whole lot of heart. Otherwise, the other two wouldn't love and respect him as much as they clearly do.

Reid hurdles the back of the sofa when he returns, and lands in the spot to the left of me. The same spot he occupied during the film last night. Max remains on my right, his arm slung protectively around my shoulder.

"Can't believe you put me on hold, but let this guy take you all the way to a big O."

"Reid!" Max grumbles.

"What?"

"She feels bad about it, so stop making your mouth go and making it worse."

"Ariel?" He nuzzles his head against my shoulder. "You know I'm only teasing, right? Any right-minded woman would choose to do Max. Of course, they'd also choose to do me."

"Maybe she doesn't want to have sex with you." Wynter's returned. There's no space for him on the couch, so he rests against the side of the armchair by the fireplace.

"She totally wants to have sex with me," Reid retorts. "Don'tcha, Ariel?"

I wish that the sofa would develop sentience and devour me.

Wynter rolls his eyes and releases a groan. "Seriously?"

"What?" asks Max.

"She fucking wants to, that's what."

"Duh!" Max responds to Wynter. "Obviously. She's hot for you, too. How did you miss this?"

Wynter's brows crook sceptically. He squints at me. "That true, Iris?"

"I'm game." Reid inches closer, so that our thighs brush.

His present invasion of my space gives me an opportunity to avoid answering Wynter's direct question. Wanting something and confessing it out loud are two entirely different things.

"How dirty do you want to get, sea siren? Threeway? Fourway? DP? DVP?"

I keep my mouth firmly closed.

"No need to be shy about it."

"Do you think I can pay a plastic surgeon to sew his mouth shut?" Wynt asks Max.

Max, reassuringly, still has his arm around my shoulders.

"I'm sure you can find a dodgy enough hack somewhere who'll do it for the dough, but don't because then I'll have to do backing vocals."

Wynter shrugs. "That ain't gonna be an issue in a few. Six days and we're defunct, guys. Give it twelve months and no one will even remember we existed."

"That's not true." Apparently, I've found my tongue faced with the prospect of my favourite band dissolving. "Have a little more faith in your fans, please. We're out there. We're waiting and we're excited. We're not going anywhere, and there's no reason for you to either."

"Oh, you do have a voice."

I nod. "Can't you get outside help?"

"For his *lyric-i-tis*?" Reid asks.

"Plenty bands use songwriters, right?" I look to the three of them for confirmation. I have no insider knowledge of the music industry, but I know there are plenty of artists who don't write their material.

Wynter draws his lips into a rueful pucker. "Been there, tried that."

The response is more tempered and less knee jerk than I anticipate. He sighs, then crosses his ankles and sinks into a cross-legged sitting position, back to the side of the armchair. "Either they don't get our sound, or they deliberately set out to distort it and turn it into something so trite and cringey, it makes our tackles shrivel."

"So, what happens in six days?"

Wynter rakes his hands through his blond hair in frustration. "It's how long we have to deliver something before the label pulls the plug and drop us."

"Or worse," Max adds in a low grumble. "Decides to release the subpar atrocity the hack they hired produced."

"Is it really that bad?"

"Worse," Reid sighs. "It's the pits."

"That man was a fucking butcher. I don't care if he's an industry darling, what he did to our sound was a crock of shit." Clearly agitated, Max withdraws his arm from around my shoulder, a space Reid immediately fills.

As my gaze ping-pongs between them, it's obvious there's a consensus of agreement and inevitability about their demise.

They've helped me. Maybe it's time I helped them. "What can I do?"

"Not a damn thing, Iris." The way Wynter says it puts a crack right through my heart. We might not see eye to eye, but he's tragic in this moment, and I want nothing more than to offer him comfort in any way that I can.

Reid shakes his head.

But Max peers at me hopefully. "You don't happen to be a songwriting genius or an award-winning poet, do you?"

"'fraid not. I did once win a slam poetry contest in primary school, but I'm thinking that doesn't count."

"Snap," he claims. "Mine was about my pet dog, what was yours about?"

"Flesh-eating zombies."

"Producer friend?" Reid asks, nibbling on a chipped, black-painted fingernail. I let him down with a rueful head shake. His shoulders sag only for him to plaster on a grin, and say, "So, shag, then, Iris? While I'm still a hot commodity."

"Stop it." Wynter chucks a cushion at him, which hits him in the face. "She doesn't want to shag you."

Not actually true, but I'm not about to risk turning the conversation back in that direction. There's still a knot of tension in my stomach, and butterflies in my brain keen on reminding me that shagging three friends is not reasonable behaviour. At best, it makes me a groupie, at worst, something far less pleasant.

"We should try to work something out," Max says.

"Yeah." Wynter droops from the shoulders. It's like he's determinedly folding himself up small, so the universe doesn't notice him, and the bad things romp off to elsewhere and juicier pickings.

Reid tears at his hair, leaving the curling strands standing on end. "Guys? Please. We really gonna spend another night staring at the studio walls? 'Cause I have to say, I'd rather spend it shagging Iris. I feel that'd be more productive, and possibly inspirational. Definitely aspirational."

Wynter raises his head to shake it at the fool. "Iris, who has yet to even hint at the possibility that she wants to shag you? Might want to consult her on that before making any plans."

Reid nudges my cheek with his nose. "You want to, don't you, hun? Besides, aren't those the unwritten rules? If you shag one of us, you have to shag us all."

"They're not unwritten rules, they're your imagination getting the better of you."

"At least mine's working."

That was low. I wince on Wynter's behalf.

Wynter's mouth has tightened into a lemon pucker. Max, the eternal mediator, pushes onto his feet, and sticks a hand out to help Wynter rise. "Let's just go jam for a while, guys. Iris, come with. Maybe having an audience will inspire us."

I'm not about to say no to a private Lucidity show. Max gives me a hand onto my feet too.

"Am I okay to take some pictures? Ric loaned me a camera."

"Sure, just don't get in the way," Wynter replies.

Reid mutters under his breath about how much nicer the evening could be. Meanwhile, I jog up the stairs to fetch the camera. When I come back down, Reid and Wynter have already left, but Max is waiting for me. "Don't let Reid pressure you, even if you want it. And don't take this as me trying to stop you. I'm just saying, do things on your terms, not his."

Wise words, and certainly ones I'm going to endeavour to live by. Although, I'm still having trouble wrapping my head around the idea that it's okay to have all three flavours of ice-cream at once, and not having to choose from strawberry, vanilla, or chocolate.

"Do you really not have anything?" I ask as we cross the plaza. They must have something, if they've spent time with a producer.

"Some," he squeezes my hand. "Actually, plenty, but Wynt's lost faith in it after what happened with..." He shakes his head. "He's started believing he's as shit as that bastard made our stuff sound. He did a real hatchet job on him, made him doubt his ability, which sucks, because the demo versions we did were ace. Raw, certainly, but ace."

"Wanker," I say, which provokes a smile. "So, you're saying you all had faith in them before this producer guy soured shit?"

"I still do now. So does Reid. They're great songs, it's just the production that imbecile put on them that fucked them up. Oh, and his insistence on tampering with the lyrics. He didn't understand nuance."

"So, if you went back to how you envisaged them originally...?"

"Convince Wynter, not me. I'm already there."

We reach the studio, and he pauses to hold the

door open for me. "What if you played them for me? I could be your test audience."

He scratches his chin as he ushers me forward into the open plan space. "Maybe."

I'm not sure what I was expecting a recording studio to look like. The room we enter is not dissimilar to the one we just left, only minus the fireplace. There's a duo of couches, and a large meeting style table with chairs. A tiny kitchenette sits off to one side, and a couple of doors lead off to uncharted areas. The walls of what is clearly a converted barn house a score of risqué Alaric Liddell originals of bands current and past. Some of them put fire into my cheeks.

It makes the camera I'm holding into a grenade again.

What the hell am I supposed to shoot that's going to impress Ric Liddell?

"Loos. Studio." Max drags me onwards through the right-hand door to where I gather the magic is supposed to happen. It's a narrow room lined with equipment, including a huge deck of buttons and sliders that'd be at home in the cockpit of a spaceship. A further door leads into a room visible through a huge window. Wynter and Reid are already in there plugging in amps and shouldering instruments. On the wall behind them is a printed sign that reads,

There's a doodle beneath it of entwined figures with a huge red cross drawn over it. Someone has stuck another note beneath:

YES, THAT FUCKING MEANS YOU, GEIST. DO NOT TEST ME, UNLESS YOU WANT YOUR ARSE ACROSS THE WORLD'S MEDIA.

There are tally marks beneath.

I assume Geist is Xane Geist, the lead singer of goth metal superstars, Black Halo. There were rumours of sightings of them in this area up until quite recently. Seems they were true.

Reid catches me looking at the sign and shouts, not that I can hear him thanks to the soundproofing. He makes some wild gestures that get the gist across. Rough translation, you and me, babe. Let's add a score to the tally.

I wave back no, but I'm not sure he sees it, as Wynter slaps him around the back of the head, and mouths something that might be, "She chose Max, cretin."

Max, also an observer of this, waits until the pair of them are silent, then hits a button on the console, which allows us to hear what's inside the room. He pulls a swivel chair over for me to park my bum in, then heads on through to join his bandmates, following a reminder not to touch anything.

I watch them jam for a bit. Eventually, riffs and drums coalesce into songs from their first album. When they play my favourite tune, I get up and sing and dance along. Seems to me they need reminding that they have genuine fans out there who love their stuff.

They keep playing, and I pick up the camera. I can't really focus on the guys that well, due to the glass between me and them, but I take some shots of pretty reflections and the working environment with them in the background.

They've been playing for thirty to forty minutes, when Max starts throwing meaningful looks my way. There's an intercom button, clearly labelled. I press it. "How about giving me something I've not heard yet?"

"We could do *Troubled Introduction*," Max suggests, and Reid nods. I realise they've been planning this. Rather than waiting for Wynter, Max starts tapping out the rhythm on his drum kit.

Wynter stands frozen, but Reid joins in after a moment, playing the main riff, and eventually, Wynter begins fingering the fretboard of his bass. Man, it's hooky as hell. That bass especially. It roots its way right under my skin and twangs all the nerve endings there. Where I expect the vocals to start, Wynter stays quiet. Both Reid and Max shoot him looks, but none of them stop playing.

"Come on, man," Reid mutters. "It's just Iris. She's not going to crucify us, even if it's dreck, which it isn't."

They loop the instrumentation. When they get there, Wynter croaks a few hesitant words. By the time they've done a third repeat, I'm on edge, my teeth aching in my jaw from clenching them so hard. But, oh, my God, there's no respite when this time he finds his voice and sings a whole line. He stops. Starts again, stronger. I swear, if I wasn't already half in love with them all, then I'd be so now. The lyrics delivered in that raspy tone are weighed with pure emotion. I'm literally stunned. By the end of the two-minute masterpiece, every hair on my body is standing on end. I don't hesitate in bursting through the door to let them know that.

"How? What the fuck, guys! That was amazing. You're all nuts if you think you don't have anything to record." I smack a kiss on Reid's cheek. "Sheer perfection." Deliver the same to Max. To Wynter, I say, "Please tell me you're releasing that. It'll be the biggest fucking tragedy if you don't."

"Bit hyperbolic, Iris" he mutters, but I can see that my words have affected him. There's a thaw in his eyes that paints an emerald ring about their edges.

"Seriously, Wynter." I temper my joy. I want him to know I mean this. "I think this is my new favourite from you guys. It builds on everything you delivered on your first album and does so with a punch. And if you don't think I'm serious about that then just feel." I grab his hand and hold it, so his palm is pressed to my chest. My heart is racing. It speeds even more at his touch.

"You do seem pretty excited." He rakes his teeth over his lower lip.

Good grief, Lord of the Understatement! "I'm fucking ecstatic. You're a genius. Take the compliment."

"Iris." He raises his hand so that he's cupping my cheek. "Please. Be real, eh?"

I laugh at the notion that I could convincingly fake any sort of reaction. An actress I am not. Also, his hands are seriously lovely. Slender, with agile fingers, on which he's wearing multiple rings, including one on his thumb. "What else have you got? If there's more, I want to hear it."

"*Forever in Reverse?*" Reid suggests.

Wynter winces. I feel it, as he's still holding me, but I see the flash of anguish fork through his eyes, too. I think he's about to say no. That the smog of doubt is about to surround him again and steal any sort of mental clarity about their current material.

"For me," I plead as I squeeze his fingers.

He blinks. "For you?"

"Please."

"For you?"

"For me," I agree. I tiptoe and press a kiss to his lips, and magic happens. The clouds break, and he stares at me in wonder and then... then, there's a smile. A smile that rises from within. A smile like the sun on fresh snow. It dazzles. It mesmerises. I need to capture that smile on film. Suddenly, I'm not looking at a grumpy, downtrodden man with the weight of the world on his shoulders. I'm gazing at an elven prince with the heavens in his eyes, and a melody bleeding from his fingertips.

I have enough presence of mind to take a goddamned picture of him.

"You honestly liked that last track, and you want to hear more?"

How is he so blind to his genius?

"I'm going to cry if you don't give me more. I loved it."

"Not too soppy, or … soulless."

"You know it's not any of those things." I'm sure he does, even if he's doubting himself. Deep down, he knows this is good. Has to. "It was beautiful, Wynter. And I bet it's not even the best track on the album."

He nibbles his lower lip, eyes downcast.

"No," he admits after a moment, lips betraying him, and revealing that inner deep belief I was sure was present somewhere. He coughs to clear his throat. "That is… Personally, I prefer—"

From the corner of my eye, I see Reid's grip tighten around the neck of his guitar.

"—one of the others."

"Play it, please." I'm willing to get on my knees and beg.

He takes his sweet time making a decision.

"Fucking, yeah!" Reid gasps.

Thus, I know it's going to happen, ahead of Wynter actually giving a nod. Reid can read this man in ways I can't yet.

"We're doing this?" Max asks.

Wynter gives another nod.

"Now we're talking." All the tension in Reid's body has released, and he's a shambles, vibrating like he's plugged into the amp and not his guitar.

"I need another one of these first, though. Just to make it a fair trade. Deal, Iris?"

He reels me in and slays me with a kiss that is so much more than the one I gave him. When our mouths break apart, he holds me for a long, meaningful moment, before returning his attention to the instrument suspended from the strap around his shoulders. "*Forever in Reverse.* For you, Iris. Or, as it was originally titled—. Fuck it! How it *is* titled, *Weep.*"

This time, I listen from the same room, right up close and personal, barely an arm span away from the mic he's singing into. It makes it intimate, and oh, so very visceral. Something has shifted in Wynter. I can hear it in his voice. There's a confidence to his delivery that I realise was absent before. The lack of hesitance. The sincerity that makes the track hit like a gut punch. Weeping is what I'm doing by the end. It's so beautiful, it hurts. I have goosebumps all across my body.

I take pictures. Numerous pictures, some of which are likely blurred, since I can't see properly due to my tears. The song they do after is more up tempo and optimistic. It's bound to become a fan favourite, but I'm still so in love with *Weep* that it can't compare. That doesn't stop me saying my piece. "You guys... You don't need to write anything else; you've already got what you need."

Max smiles quietly to himself. Miraculously, Reid doesn't crow, "I told you so." There's still a rebellious turn to Wynter's lips, like he's not quite ready to believe what is blatantly apparent to everyone else.

"Don't you trust my opinion?

"Not sure," he admits. "I don't exactly know you, Iris. You might have fuck awful taste. We might be the anomaly in your collection."

Way to dampen the high I was feeling.

"Do we need to exchange playlists?" If I still had my phone, I'd blare all my favourites at him for the next twenty-four hours just to prove my point, but I don't, and I'm not sure rattling off song titles is going to convince him of anything.

He doesn't want to be convinced.

He's stuck in the wallowing phase. I know what that's like. No amount of me, or anyone else dressing things up in a positive light will convince him. He needs to grow into that belief for himself. But things are shifting. He's almost there. It's in his voice. It's in the way he strides out of the studio.

Reid bounds over to me and lifts me off my feet. "You're fucking magic, Ariel." He smacks a kiss on my lips. "Tell her, Max. Tell her how awesome she is."

"He left," I say, looking to the exit.

"He played," the two men counter.

Iris

WYNTER'S STILL MISSING when we sit down to eat an evening meal. His absence leaves me agitated. It feels as if it's my fault, that I was the one pushing him, but Reid and Max don't seem concerned.

"You did us a favour, Iris. Seriously," Max reassures, as he fills my plate with honey-and miso-drizzled chicken and stacks of yummy looking veg. "Wynter will be fine. This is what he does when he needs to process. He takes time out. Don't worry, he'll come back."

Reid spears an asparagus stalk and attempts to put it in his mouth sideways. "He's probably gone for a drive."

Wait! "There are roads on this island?" Also, they have a car here.

"He'll have crossed to the mainland."

I pause, fork halfway to my mouth, then lower it to the plate again.

"You okay, Iris?" Max stops dishing up and strokes a hand through my hair.

I nod. "I guess I forgot how close home really is. Is it safe for Wynter to be randomly driving places alone?"

They both chuckle at that. "What, do you think he's going to get mobbed?"

Yes, I do.

"We still have lives, Iris. We still exist outside of the celebrity bubble. If we're together, we've more chance of being recognised, but apart, dressed as our regular selves rather than made up for the cameras, people rarely make the connection. They don't expect us to do our own shopping or fill our cars at the local petrol station. Wynter will be fine. He's probably pulled into a layby on some windy country road next to a Neolithic burial site soaking up the vibes."

It's actual easy to imagine him doing exactly that. A lone figure in the dark. The sort of person people will drive past because they think he's weird.

As Max cooked, and Wynter's not here, I help Reid with the tidying up. "I've never met three men who were so fastidious about the dishes," I say as we unload the previous load of crockery from the dishwasher ready to fill it again. They tidy religiously after every meal. There are never piles of plates by the sink, or crumbs on the worktops. It seems especially odd that chaos goblin, Reid, seems to be responsible for most of this cleanliness.

"Had it drummed into me by my nan. She always had rotas, and her sayings. It's still the first thing she says to me when she sees me, 'Are there dishes in your sink, young man?' Well, after, 'Are you eating properly? Who's washing your underwear? And if you must paint your nails, you ought to do a better job of it'."

"She sounds interesting."

He gives an enthusiastic nod. "One of the best people I've ever met."

"Tell me one of her sayings?"

He doesn't have to think about it. "'Messy house blues, we'll clean and soothe.' If shit was going down when I was a kid, especially when I was a teenager, she'd say that and then hand me a scouring brush then we'd do the kitchen floor together while we talked over shit. It weirdly always worked, with the added boon of a clean floor, or bath, or windows. Pretty sure I scoured her whole house at least a dozen times, and painted most of it twice, too."

"Tried it as an approach with Wynter?"

"Yup. I wound up wearing the bucket."

It takes me a second to realise he means Wynter upended soapy water over him.

"What else did your nan teach you?"

"You mean beside how to play guitar?" He nods. "She was a music teacher." His lips elongate as he thinks. "Let's see. Sharing is caring."

Clearly, I'm naïve, because I initially think he means this in the usual sense. It becomes obvious he doesn't when he takes the pan from my hand and sets it aside, and presses his hand to my palm instead, then laces our fingers. "So... I lost out to Max, eh?"

"Reid. Oh, God. I'm sorry. He kissed me and—"

"You liked it."

I swallow. I can hear his disappointment clogging up his throat.

"I liked it when you did it, too."

"But I've missed my chance, right? Went off half-cocked and got myself disqualified from the running as a result."

"Reid. That's not how..."

"Sorry, I can't keep it up." His sorrowful expression cracks into mirth. "Max doesn't have a possessive bone in his body. Bet he even told you about past us, so you'd know he wasn't erecting barriers between you and Wynter and me 'cause of you two shagging."

My insides do a funny sort of belly flop. "He did mention something to that effect."

"So?"

"So?"

"Wanna come upstairs with me after we've finished up here?"

"To do what?"

He raps on my head with the flat of his palm. "Iris, I feel you're not keeping up. To give one another orgasms, obviously."

"That's awfully direct."

He lifts his shoulders in his defence. "I'm a direct sort of guy. What's the point in obfuscating. I want you. I think you want me—"

Do I?

"—Max isn't going to get upset about it, and I'll tell you what, I'll throw in some camera time as a sweetener. You, me, that brute of a camera Ric's loaned you, and not a stitch of clothing. I'll even sign waiver papers so you can use them however you want."

How am I supposed to resist? I finish up loading the dishwasher, while Reid runs a cloth over the work surfaces. Max is snoozing on the sofa as we pass, his long legs draped over the arm. We head upstairs hand in hand.

"Are you sure he's not going to mind?"

"You want to wake him and ask?"

I don't. He looks peaceful, his mouth partly open, and his expression turned all soft. I know what his answer will be. It's not a problem, Iris. It's the norms the rest of society imposes on us that are niggling me, not Max's opinion, or worries over hurting his feelings.

"Your place or mine?" Reid asks when we reach the upper landing.

"Yours." I want to see Reid Rushmore's personal space almost as much as I want to see him stripped bare of his tatty clothes.

His room is tucked into the eaves, with a dormer window on one side. Still, the roof is low enough even I worry about banging my head on some of the beams. It's clean and yet chaotic. He's obviously been living out of his suitcase. It stands open, set on top of a sea chest, a jumble of clothes hanging out of it. There's a small desk cum dresser before the window, looking out towards the fort, a high-backed armchair next to a small circular coffee table overflowing with electronic devices – laptop, chargers, a handheld games console and a charging pad for his phone. And a second chair that looks as if it's made of macrame suspended from the ceiling beams. What it takes me a minute to realise is that there's something obvious missing.

"Where's the bed?"

"There isn't one."

"Then where do you sleep?"

His gaze flicks to a rolled-up mat in the corner.

"On the floor?" Did he give his bed up to me, when they rescued me off the beach?

"Sometimes I share with Wynter. Depends on the mood."

"Let's go next door."

"Iris." He grabs my hand. "Let's stay here." He backs me up against the door, and holding me by the chin, kisses me in a flighty way that barely allows our lips to touch. "Ever had sex in a swing before?"

"Um, no."

"Want to?"

I do, now he's suggested it. I always loved the sensation in my belly flying back and forth used to produce. I realise now, it was a form of arousal.

"Are we talking about the string contraption over there?"

"It's secure, I promise. I've tested it. A lot."

"How would that work?"

He cocks his head. Gives the hanging chair an assessing glance. "You swinging, me standing, I think."

"You think." I'm busy trying to envisage this pose. I can. All too well, if I'm honest. Me tilted backwards, my legs pulled up into a W shape but also splayed apart. Reid's hands around my hips.

His cock perfectly aligned. The damn chair even looks as if it's hanging at precisely the right height.

"You'll be able to sit back and enjoy and let me do all the work." He winks. "Hell, you'll probably have your hands free enough to snap the before, during, and aftermath."

"Photograph you while we're fucking?" I blurt it, even as the idea wraps itself around my synapses and my inner muscles clench. More than anything, I realise, even more than the notion of the swing, I'm obsessed with the idea.

Such an intimate moment, but will the camera make it clinical, or will it become an extension of my desire for this man? This beautiful, unruly, joker of a man, with his hair that determinedly curls at the ends, his scruff-covered jaw, and chiselled Adonis belt.

"Do you really want that much of yourself out in the world?"

"Why not? I can't be with a thousand, ten thousand, a million fans, but I can give them fantasy fodder that maybe makes their days a little brighter."

That seems very generous of him. "You don't mind being objectified like that?"

"Why the hell wouldn't I want people to look at images of me and think, Fuck! I really want to fuck that man? It's the ultimate compliment."

I can follow his logic, even if I don't entirely agree. I guess that's why I like being the one holding the camera, rather than the object of its focus.

"So, a few photos to get us warmed up?" Reid

steps back a few paces, giving me room to focus the camera. He pulls his T-shirt off, tugging from the neck in the way that guys do, only he does it in slow motion. It's hard to say if he's giving me time to capture the moment, or if it's because he's a monumental tease. Either way, I eat it up. His body is all lines and shadows, and strategically placed ink. I love the way his muscles make a patchwork of his lower torso. A thin trail of hair, a lighter tone to that on his head, forms a marker between left and right that compels the gaze downwards.

"Fly?" he teases, finger and thumb coyly curled to his softly parted lips. I realise I don't just want to capture him here. I want to see him sprayed with sea surf, sand clinging to the backs of his thighs and his bare arse. I want to see him stretched across a rumpled bed, clutching his guitar, and more... Scenario after scenario floods my mind, even as I capture him in the here and now.

Watching him undress is like being taken on a journey. The way he rolls off his socks. The way he takes one leg out of his jeans before the other and shields his assets from my view with a carefully positioned arm and hand after shedding his boxer briefs.

He turns, flashing me an arse that's the equal of his abs. I'm obsessed with the divot right at the top of his cleft.

Reid, reaches back, inviting me to follow, and we shuffle over to the chair, where he demonstrates how I should recline in it. I take pictures from every angle. Pictures of bits of him that the public have never seen and probably shouldn't. Some of these images, I've already decided, will be just for me. Mine to remember him by when this time is over. There's already a clock ticking down on our time left together.

This is not the real world. It's time out from that.

I pause, while I figure out what comes next. Where to pitch my hopes and dreams.

"Let me hold the camera for you a moment while you undress."

"You're not going to do it?"

"Uh-uh! I peeled you free of sodden things when you first washed up. Now I want to watch you get naked for me."

I'm only wary because he's holding a camera in his hand, and my skin is still a patchwork of yellows, browns, purples, and greens. The bruises don't hurt per se, but some areas are still tender when they're touched.

"It's okay, Ariel. I won't love you through the lens. I'd rather do that without any filters between us."

At least he doesn't look at me as if I'm a wounded bird. Rather, his tongue skims his teeth as his hot gaze wanders over my body, and he makes appreciative noises in the back of his throat.

"Well, hello there, beautiful. Would you like to get into your perch?"

I'd like to imagine I do so gracefully.

Reid closes in once I'm seated. His fingers skim up my arms, then down to my breasts. He bows his head and suckles my nipples. His hair tickles my skin. I breathe in his scent, salt, and skin, with a touch of peppery shower gel.

"Hm, remember me, girls?"

They obligingly pucker in response to this greeting. His attention lowers to my hips. One palm gets splayed across my tummy. Then, his fingers are in his mouth and he's wetting them, pushing through my curls to the true target of his interest.

"Touch me," he breathes into my ear. He leaves me holding the camera one-handed as he guides the other to his cock. He's semi-hard but fills out quickly as my palm encompasses him. I let out a groan, as I move instinctively. He's not the first man I've masturbated. He is the first I've touched while recording the process.

I keep going, stroking him, skin on skin, while he does the same to me. "Like this?" he asks. "Or better, like this?"

Anyway, and every way. His touch is like lightning. It sends volt after volt of crackling energy through my synapses. I never want him to stop. I know I'm going to come soon if he doesn't let up a little.

"I want to come while you're inside me," I say.

Hazel eyes crinkle at the corners. "Inside you right here." His index finger circles my entrance, then dips into the well of moisture gathered there.

"Yes, please."

"Sweet Ariel, I can't deny you anything."

He's a charmer, no mistaking. We wriggle and shift. Soft laugh, and moan. Reid lifts my legs. I hook them around his back and return to watching him through the viewfinder. There's so much I don't want to miss.

Reid strokes me as the swing rocks gently back and forth. He bends and unfolds one of my legs so that he can run his hands along its length, then kiss the same pathway. His breath tickles in the moments before he tastes me. His tongue is a little rough, but he knows what he's doing. It gets harder and harder to keep a part of myself detached and focused on making a record of our actions. "You're still teasing me."

"Just making certain I'm not short-changing you."

It's all unhurried. I lick my lips while I watch him roll on a condom. "Just to be safe. I know you've an implant."

How the fuck does he know that?

"Left arm." He nods in that direction. "There's a bump where it is."

Okay, no one has ever noticed it before. Reid Rushmore is more observant than most. He goes back to rubbing my swollen clit, making me wetter and increasingly breathless. I'm skating closer and closer. Body tensing.

I record the very moment he notches his cock inside of me. I don't want to stop there, but the sensation is too much. The camera slips from my grasp, and instead of reaching for it, I reach for him. I kiss his chest, breathe in the mixed scent of our arousal. Reid pulls the swing towards him, and I slide onto him. He holds us there joined. Kisses every part of me he can reach. My skin prickles and comes alive. I'm waiting for the swooping sensation that comes as his cock slides out. I want it so badly, I start arching my back. It's a strain for him too. He holds on. Prolongs our joint agony, but eventually, he gives in to the sensations we both crave.

Reid fucks me long and well, and far into the night.

We rut and we wriggle.

Each time I come I'm flooded with warmth and grow a little more infatuated with him. His teeth find my shoulder when he finishes for the second time. "I'm already half in love with you, mermaid girl," he sighs.

He knows every inch of me by the time we retire to my room and the comfort of the bed. I know every inch of him, too. The divot from an accident he sustained aged twelve on his left butt cheek. The long wings of his shoulder blades and the ladder of his spine. Even the triangle of golden-brown freckles that occupy that space between his balls and his tightly furled pucker.

When we wake, Wynter is back. He stands in the half open doorway looking at us, limbs entangled and poking out from beneath the equally tangled and rumpled duvet.

Reid stirs and stretches an arm out towards him. "Space for one more."

"I need some kip."

"Space for one more," Reid repeats.

I expect Wynter to stalk off. It shocks me into wakefulness when he instead steps into the room. He undresses unhurriedly, down to black slip briefs, and climbs into bed on the far side of Reid, who slings an arm around his friend.

"Where did you go?"

"Just for a drive."
"Tide catch you out?"
"For a while."
"Anyone bother you?"
He doesn't answer that one immediately. Reid wriggles and props himself up on his elbow. "Wynter."
"No one bothered me, but there are posters up, asking if anyone's seen your mermaid girl."

11
IRIS

I OUGHT TO have predicted that my absence would be reported. Cathy might not realise that her son is a monster, but she's not made from the same stuff as him. She's a regular human being with a kind heart and an entrenched set of sensibilities. Of course, she'd be worried if I didn't come home, nor answer when she tried to reach me. I'm only assuming the latter. My phone is presumably at the bottom of the sea, or maybe it's been found by an early morning jogger or dog walker, or a family paddling in the rock pools left behind when the tide is low.

I ought to let her know that I'm safe.

I contemplate this, while the guys work in the studio. A breakthrough of sorts has been made, but Wynter still requires regular reminders. The cajoling eats up both Reid and Max's time. Much of mine too, although I learn to temper any form of hyperbole while speaking to him, as he perceives it as blowing smoke up his arse.

It ought to be as simple as typing a message to let Cathy know that I'm alive and well. I ought to say, pack up my things and have them shipped to this address, even if I can't explain to her why I can't come back and collect them myself.

But it isn't simple.

I'm not a walking encyclopaedia of phone numbers. Like everyone, I store them on my phone. Also, I don't want Harrison to learn I'm less than a mile away. Whether I make Cathy aware of what happened or not, I don't trust her not to discuss it with him. If someone told me my child had done something reprehensible, I feel I'd want to hear them deny it. I'm sure it's what Cathy will do, and then he'll know I'm alive, that there's been contact. That there's the possibility I might land him in shit.

I can't call her.

I can't leave her in limbo.

What to do?

I don't know what to do.

Reach her via social media?

I send her a DM the following night from Reid's phone as we sit at Blackwater's restaurant, along with a picture of myself, so she knows that it's me.

Met someone. I'm okay. You don't need to look for me.

We're eating out because the guys recorded the drums for four tracks today, thus Max is exhausted. He was literally dripping with sweat when he came out of the studio.

I've never been to Blackwater's before. It's every bit as posh as I imagined. Most of the seating is outside beneath a wooden canopy, that's draped in twinkling fairy lights.

I lean against Max as Reid feeds me oysters. At least a couple of them end up on the floor. I'm not sure I like them all that much; too briny, too gelatinous, but it's fun with the guys. Even Wynter has thawed a little. He bends double with laughter when Reid's reaction to lashing himself with spaghetti and painting tomatoey stripes across his white shirt is to starfish his limbs and unwittingly upend the candelabra sitting on our table so that it burns a hole in the tablecloth.

The staff here must be used to musicians. They don't break a sweat as they replace everything, and no one says, "Are you the guys from Lucidity?" Although, a couple of women follow Wynter back from the loos and beg him for autographs.

All three of them sign T-shirts. Max draws the line at bits of skin. Reid happily signs the blonde girl's tits when she flashes him.

"Take a photograph," the women insist, pushing phones into my hands.

I take obligatory snaps of them preening next to their idols. Days ago, I might have been them.

"Sign breasts often?" I ask on the walk back to the studio complex.

"Are you jealous? It's fine, Ariel. I'll happily squiggle my name and claim one of yours, too."

"Which one are you claiming?" Wynter asks.

I'm still routinely discombobulated by him.

Reid weighs up his options by pulling me into a hug and groping me. "I think the left... No, the right one. Definitely the right one. You want to stamp your mark on the other one, man?"

Wynter lets out a sigh through his slender nose. "Sharpie isn't how I like to claim my property."

"Yeah, but man, it's a little early in the relationship for you to be pissing all over her."

A) What relationship? And B) "No one is pissing on me, ever."

"Can I come all over you?" Reid drops his head onto my shoulder, which makes walking next to impossible. He's too tall, and his head must weigh as much as his body.

I roll my eyes. "Like you haven't already."

He catches my earlobe between his teeth. It sends little sparks shooting down through my neck to where his hand is still possessively holding my breast. "Can I come all over you again?"

I consider. Letting him stew for a heartbeat. "Yeah, okay. Take me home to bed you mighty stallion." He gallops in front of me making horse noises and pats his rear signalling for me to climb astride.

I do a run and a jump, then he piggybacks me all the way to bed.

12

IRIS

OVER THE NEXT streak of day, the guys work in the studio, and I catalogue the process of them recreating their sound and recording new demo versions of their tracks. The hours are long and often fraught. I spend alternate nights with Reid and Max. Wynter sometimes looks at me with a question burning in his eyes, but he never says anything or makes any sort of move. There's no reprising of the kiss he gave me in the studio after the first time I heard them play live. Nor does he climb into bed with Reid and me again. I think Reid sleeps with him on the nights he's not with me.

I continue to avoid thinking too deeply about this arrangement, which is probably a mistake, not to mention foolish, but I'm afraid of what I'll unearth if I do. Plus, there's a deadline on all of this, anyway. I don't want to say goodbye, but I know goodbye is coming, and I refuse to be that girl. The one who expects more than she should of what's actually there.

I'm a fun distraction, and they're a fantasy. It's not real. It's never going to be more than this. It's not forever. It doesn't matter if I wish otherwise.

The fact that their deadline is right around the corner means the tension increases as each day passes. Even Max cracks and throws his drumsticks across the room at one point.

Thursday marks Reid's turn in the sound booth. I'm idling on the couch reading while Wynter and Max man the sound deck. There's only so much time a girl can spend listening to her favourite band play the same songs, or bits of songs over again. Only so many photographs of the same thing you can take, too. I don't pretend to understand the process, only that whatever they're doing is only part of it and sound engineers and producers and mastering apparently come before the final version the public get is done. It's certainly not as simple as pressing record.

Honestly, I can't hear the difference between one version and the next most of the time. I think my hearing works differently to theirs.

Besides, this book is *durty*. I'm bookmarking the best bits to try out while I have two very willing partners. I've grown used to them. I don't want to leave them behind. I don't want them to leave me behind.

The hours tick by. It's rained incessantly all day. I haven't been outside this room in at least four hours. I need snacks. Chocolate to take away the bitterness in my brain. The breakout area needs a vending machine. I'm going to suggest Reid suggest it to Ric. I'm not going to presume to do so, but snacks would be nice, given there are no handy shops.

"Max, is there any chocolate?"

"Not in here."

Wynter signals an okay to Reid through the glass, and he puts aside his guitar and joins us in the sound booth, lifting my feet and putting them on his lap after he flops onto the couch.

He smells musky after hours of playing.

"They better be fucking happy with this, or I'm going to rip someone a new arsehole," he moans. The callouses on his fingertips weren't as pronounced before. A rough bit of skin scratches my sole as he massages my feet.

"What if we don't give them anything?"

All three of us gape at Wynter. Reid grinds his teeth, which is a truly horrible sound. Max sighs and scratches his head.

"Really, you're doubting it all again?"

"No." He stands. "Not the work. Not us. I just don't know that I trust them. They've already screwed us once. They're the ones that brought in—"

"The knob-end," Reid curses.

"Quite."

"But if we don't deliver, that's it." I've experienced many of Max's hugs now. I've never seen him look quite as much like he needed one. If he was a chibi animal, his ears would be turned down, and his eyes flooded. "Do we really want to be let go? Wynt?"

I pull my feet away from Reid. In his agitation, he's pressing too hard.

"He's got a point, man. We fought fucking hard to get to this point. I don't want to risk it all getting flushed down the pan."

"What if there's an alternative?" Wynter draws a card from his pocket. His band mates lean in for a look. It's a black and white business card, with the word Stormland across it in big bold lettering.

"They're a fraction of the size of the company we're with. It'd be taking a backwards step."

"Or a step towards freedom," Wynter suggests. "The pair of you—the three of you—have spent the last week telling me a backwards step is sometimes the right one. I think we should consider this. Really consider this. Yes, Stormland are an indie label, but they specialise in our genre. Our actual genre, not the one our current management keep trying to shoehorn us into. And we've met Harry. We know he's sound. He won't bullshit us."

"What's to say he's even interested?"

"He made us an offer before."

"Ten months ago," Reid counters. "I don't know, man. It's risky. We'll need to think about it."

"Obviously. I'm not suggesting you don't."

Me, I wonder how long that card's been burning a hole in Wynter's pocket, and I wonder if his band mates realise his decision is already made.

"How long do you have until you have to make a decision?" I ask.

"Tomorrow evening," Max replies.

Shit! "That soon?" I swallow, as reality pinches at my flesh. When they said through to the end of the week, I'd rationalised that as until Monday morning, not Friday evening. I've hardly any time left with them at all.

13

WYNTER

I GET AS far as the sea wall, to the stretch that surely has my butt cheeks imprinted on it by now. The tide is on its way in again. It's still drizzling. The chill of the wet brickwork seeps through my jeans and chills my arse. A week on from finding Iris, and my heart is still in turmoil. Not for the same reason though. I get it, it's a risk I'm asking Max and Reid to take, but staying with our current representation is impossible for me.

There's no trust left. I can feel my hair standing on end from considering the possibility.

I have considered it.

We need to talk it out. The guys need to understand that if they opt to stay, I'm not staying with them. Even if it's a no from Stormland. I'd rather go back to being a nobody than endure more of the shit I've faced these past months.

I hear footsteps and look up, half expecting to see Iris. It's Reid. His brown hair is increasingly curly thanks to the sea air. Not even the rain can flatten it. He comes to a halt before me and rubs his arms against the wind rolling in off the sea. "You dressed that up as an option, but it's not an option, is it?"

Slowly, I shake my head.

"Shit!" He slumps onto the wall beside me as he rubs his mouth and jaw. "Are you sure?"

"I can't..."

"We've a whole fucking album's worth of material."

"I know. I'm not saying that you and Max—"

"We're not splitting up." He stands again, to labour that point. "We're not, Wynter. We're in this for the long haul. Shit. Oh, fucking shit!" he howls into the sea. Then, he about turns and sits alongside me, blowing hot air into his hands.

"When did you decide?"

I tug my jacket around me. "It's been bubbling away since—"

"That bastard screwed things."

"Pretty much, but I... I didn't believe we had anything to offer anyone else until after we played *Weep* to Iris. Those fuckers don't deserve us, Reid. They don't. They don't deserve me."

He blows a long breath out of his mouth, then he's up and marching across the plaza like he's about to storm our current label's HQ and lob Molotovs around. At around the halfway point, he about turns and comes back to me.

"So, Stormland. That's who you want? You've researched this?"

I nod. I've turned the possibility over every which way. I don't need to give him the spiel. He knows who Stormland are as well as I do. They're a boutique outfit. Independent. Owned and run by Harry Storm. They courted us back in the day, before we were signed, and made a second offer last June. I think all three of us have lamented not signing with them in the first place at some point.

"So, what, we contact them and see if they bite?"

That's pretty much the gist.

What's more, I find I'm actually grinning at the prospect of it. "Moving labels will give us a clean start. We can hack off all the shit and leave it behind."

"What if they feel we've swung too far away from their brand? What if they're not interested."

"We convince them we're ready to swing back again, and prove it with the new stuff. And why wouldn't they be fucking interested?" I find my feet, my nerves thrumming with excitement and a pinch of pissed off. I'm done with being downtrodden. I'm done with the self-doubt. "We've an album ready to go, Reid. It's a fucking good album."

He nods, digs his teeth into his lip as he grips my shoulder and squeezes. "About fucking time. Wasn't sure you were ever going to rip the gloom filter away. It is good. It's so fucking good. It's going to be huge."

"Yeah. It is. We're going to make it fucking huge." I'm not sure when I started believing that, but I believe it now wholeheartedly. All we need to do is ditch our current representation.

Reid fishes his phone out of his back pocket. It's a sleek affair. Cost more than twice our monthly rent on the halfway decent flat we used to share. It wasn't so long ago his devices were held together with hope and sticky tape. He upgraded them, just not his everyday wardrobe.

"It's quarter to midnight," I point out. "Hardly the time to call anyone."

"So, I won't call." He flashes one of his dimpled grins. The same grin that convinced me to befriend him as we stood under a bus shelter together five years ago.

"Besides, I'm messaging a guy who manages bands. Do you really think he keeps regular hours? Even if he does, he doesn't have to respond right away."

"You're calling...messaging, Harry Storm?"

"Why delay?" Reid's thumbs race across the phone keys. "There. Sent. I attached *Weep*." It's such a Reid move. He's unpredictable but decisive. Which is how I know he's already deeply committed to Iris. He and Max both are already half in love with her, if not wholly smitten. Me...I'm a little jealous I'm not part of their fledgling polycule.

"It's being read." He offers me a cagey grin. I refuse to get my hopes up, as I watch the clouds scuttering across the gibbous moon.

Okay, my expectations are sky high, and my stomach is in my throat.

The rain finally stops.

Reid jumps in a puddle.

"And we have a response."

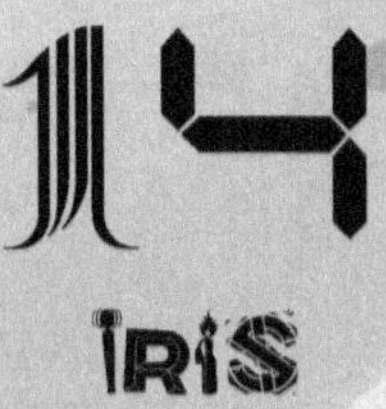

IRIS

TIME SPEEDS UP, so that the next twelve hours pass in the blink of an eye. I sat awake most of the night, and consequently slept away most of the morning.

They're in the studio again when I find them, locking down a few loose ends so they have what they need ready for their chat with Harry Storm, now a confirmed date inked onto the calendar.

At 2pm, they pre-empt the expected chewing-out by their label and call their company assigned manager.

"We're done," Wynter tells him. I'm sure the guy would be disturbed if he could see the look on Wynter's face as he says it. It's way too gleeful for what ought to be a heavy moment.

"What do you mean you're done?"

"I mean we don't have any material for you. We're not going to have any new material for you."

"You know the conseq—"

"Yeah, we get it. We understand. It's a bust. It's for the best."

The guy is clearly bamboozled by this. "You realise it's game over."

"We get it," Reid says, unable to keep his mouth shut any longer.

"How long until the contract terminates?" Wynter asks, waving at Max to keep Reid under control.

"I'll send it upstairs the moment the call ends. Expectations were set in stone when they agreed to pay for the studio time. If you don't keep your end, then you can't expect leniency."

"No. No, we wouldn't expect that. It's perfectly reasonable."

I'm sure that when this guy sends his report upstairs, it'll read as him having terminated the relationship, because he doesn't seem able to wrap his head around the fact that they're not putting up a fight.

By early evening, Lucidity are no longer part of the Chinchilla Group. They need to vacate the studio complex by midday tomorrow.

15

WYNTER

I T DOESN'T TAKE me long to pack up the couple of bass guitars I have with me. I leave Max disassembling his drum kit and help Reid wrestle a copious number of leads into boxes. He's down, which is why he turns the task into a circus. In typical Reid fashion, he doesn't say *why* he's down, he just makes endless busy work for himself.

"Just tell her you don't want it to end."

"Thought I had already."

Which means he hasn't, not really, not in an actual heart-to-heart serious conversation, only in an offhanded, hyperbolic Reid fashion. 'Stay with me to the end of time, while I kiss every inch of your skin six times over'; that sort of shit. I know him well enough to realise that means he's ready for the long haul.

Not sure Iris does.

"It's probably for the best," he sighs from his balls. "You don't like her anyway."

"Don't go pinning this on me. I never said that."

He cracks a grin, throws an arm around my shoulder, and proceeds to muck up my hair. "Ahh, you do like her. I knew it. Called it." He smacks a kiss on my cheek. "We can be all polycule-lier together. I want both my lovers to get on. It opens up the possibilities, you know..."

"Except we're leaving."

He drops the lead he was coiling, which unravels and whips him across the midriff. "Fucker." He wrestles it into submission as if it's a snake. "It's not just me. Max tried too. She's not hearing us." He turns on the sad boy face again and makes sorrowful eyes at me. "I'll do all your laundry for you, for a month... six months."

"I'm good thanks. I can do my own."

"Please fix this, Wynter. Please. You're the fix-it guy. I know you can do it. Please."

I want to throttle him. We wind up kissing instead.

IRIS IS WANDERING the shoreline when I come back from moving things across to our van. I watch her attempt to skip stones with limited success.

This is madness.

Her out here, and Reid and Max inside moping. Fuck. I told Reid I categorically wasn't going to do this, but I can't deal with this much moseying about being pathetic.

I crunch across the noisy shingle towards her, which instantly causes her to turn her head.

"Come to show me how it's done?" She offers me the chunky pebble from her palm.

"Not something I've mastered." I do know that you're supposed to use flatter stones. I hunt around and find one, along with a chunk of sea glass I offer to her.

"I'll be out of your hair tomorrow." She tries to make it sound jocular and not as if her heart is rupturing at the thought of leaving. "Sorry that I got in the way."

"What are you doing, Iris?"

"Skipping stones."

"I don't mean that. I mean the 'Sorry I got in the way'. We're way past this. You're the reason we have a future that's worth pursuing. If you hadn't arrived, our world would be fucking grim right now. Either we'd have been dropped with no hope of scoring another deal, or worse, we'd have been still fucking signed to Chinchilla and being strongarmed into releasing that utter bunch of toss their guy produced."

She accepts this with her head bowed, teeth indenting her lip. "I'm glad it worked out for you all."

It hasn't worked out, yet. We still have to convince Harry, but I believe in what we have. Enough to be optimistic.

"Why is everyone around here so shit at communicating?" I mutter it under my breath, but I mean for her to hear me. She looks up, startled. "Reid doesn't want it to end. Max doesn't want it to end. You don't want it to end. So why the fuck are you ending it?"

Her mouth drops open. Tears well in her eyes. Angry tears. Frustrated tears. "It won't last, out there. How can it. People will—"

Any phrase that starts with that sort of phrasing is always a reflection of internal fucking fears. I know. I've spent the last six months engaged in that sort of thinking.

"Fuck people. What do you want, Iris?"

She opens her mouth. Closes it again.

I try and fail to skim a stone. *Plop*! "Okay, ideal world time. Humour me. If you could have anything you want to happen tonight, tomorrow, what would that be?"

It takes her a while, but eventually she admits in the smallest of voices. "I'd leave with the three of you, and—"

"What's stopping that from happening?"

"Peop—"

"No." I abandon any further attempts at stone skipping and shake my head. "Not people. You. The only person stopping it from happening is you."

Heat blooms in her cheeks as if I've struck her with more than words. "It's not..."

I hold my ground. "Iris, why the fuck not? And if you're about to respond with some bollocks about what other people think, then don't. The only people who get to have a say in the matter are the ones involved."

"I can't date all three members of Lucidity out in the real world."

Big assumption, in more than one way. "You asking me out, mermaid girl?"

16

Iris

I'M AN IDIOT. "Wynter, you don't even like me."

"Really? That old chestnut again." His glass-green eyes are alight with a sort of inner fire I've not seen before. It makes him nearly unrecognisable. He seems so... so uncontained. It makes me realise how broken he's been. Now, the real him is peeping through. "I never said that, Iris."

"Your body language for the last week has."

"My body language sometimes lies. I lie. It's easier than being rejected." He crooks one of those devilishly sharp brows as if to challenge me on that point. Of course he fears rejection. I'm familiar with the songs now. I've heard the lyrics he wrote. Lyrics in which he bares his soul.

No wonder he recoiled into himself.

"You want me? Want to be part of..." Whatever it is that Reid, Max, and I are.

"Why is that so hard to entertain?"

I don't know. I just... I'm afraid. It feels as if he's taunting me. Him and the universe, or whatever force washed me up on this beach.

He moves closer, but I splay my hand across his abs and give him a little push away.

"Cop a feel and see if he's excited, Ariel," Reid shouts from up by the seawall.

It's a joke. It's all a joke.

Reid waves at us, standing so close, but with mountains between us. He makes a rude gesture with his fist. Wynter chastises him with a finger ticking, but Reid just smirks and pushes his tongue into his cheek. "Or ditch him, and come and pogo on my stick."

"You're a crass bastard," Wynter remarks, but he surprises me by wrapping his arms around me and pulling my back against his body, so that I can feel his interest *is* real. "Is this what you want, Iris?" He speaks right into my ear, before nicking the lobe with his teeth. "Wouldn't mind a taste of what you've already given Max and Reid."

I wriggle out of his grip, leaving him sucking on his teeth.

I can't deal with him playing with my emotions. And if it is real, then... then it doesn't matter because the dream will dissolve tomorrow regardless.

After a moment, Wynter turns away. I watch him walk towards the steps and join Reid on the seawall. It's apparent from the way that he's walking and how Reids' gaze is targeted that he's uncomfortable.

Makes two of us. I just don't quite know what to do about that.

"She's got you tetchy, hasn't she?"

Wynter flips Reid a V.

"Need me to suck it better for you?"

I must make a sound, because Reid turns his impish grin on me. "That get you going, sea siren? Or are you just figuring out you're the straightest person around these parts?"

Wynter stalks off towards the house.

I scurry to catch up with Reid, and we both tumble into the living room where we find Max laying a fire. "Must you piss him off?" He nods towards the kitchen.

"Let me." Reid bounds after him. I follow Reid but stop shy of entering the kitchen when I hear them speaking.

"Come back to the lounge," I hear Reid say.

"Why?"

"So, we can talk, that's why."

I curl my fingers against my mouth, ears perked to pick up the reply.

"She's not interested."

"Should you be eavesdropping?" Max wraps his arms around me from behind.

"I screwed up, Max. Wynter was trying to be real with me, and I...I rejected him."

He squishes me inside one of his weighty embraces.

"Do you want to come upstairs with me?" Reid is propositioning Wynter. He's trying to close the wound I've thoughtlessly inflicted with an alternate plug of affection.

"Think your mermaid girl might have something to say about that."

"Probably yes, please, and thank you, I'll have some of that," Reid predicts.

He's not wrong. I'd pay to see that. I'd pay to photograph it.

Fuck it. I want this. I do.

Wynter's right. The only person getting in my way is me. It doesn't matter what Lucidity's fan base think, or the press, or the world. It doesn't matter what the lady in the corner shop thinks, or the guy in the garage, or Harrison—. It *especially* doesn't matter what Harrison thinks. He doesn't get to dictate how I love or behave. Those are my choices to make. So why the fuck am I making decisions that are the very opposite of my own best interests?

Yes, I might get hurt. Yes, it might fall apart, but not giving it any chance at all is a way worse option. I'm a fool. All week, I've been hoping for a miracle, but I don't need one. All I need to do is believe in it, in us.

When I'd get bogged down in everything, my dad would tell me that none of it mattered. So what if I got a C in English instead of an A? So what if I needed stuff printed on pink paper to make it easily comprehensible to me? He'd say: let go of those expectations you're putting on yourself, Iris. You're building them up in your mind as things you have to do to make people accept you, but none of that is coming from them. All I want is for you to be happy, and you do that by being you. That's it. You do it by being you and not letting anyone else dictate who that is or what it is you want.

And what I want right now is them.

I may not know them perfectly after a week, but I know them enough, love them enough to know that life without them will be a thousand times less... well... everything than it'll be with them.

"She's not blind, Wynter. She knows I share your bed."

"Yeah, are you sure she knows that what happens in there isn't just sleeping?"

"She does now," I say, loudly enough to make sure they hear me. "And she's not mad about it."

"Told ya."

The pair of them emerge from the kitchen, Reid with his arm hooked around Wynter's throat. Lucidity fans would be whipped into a frenzy by this knowledge. Me? I'm almost relieved. I no longer feel like the base of some sort of fork. I don't have to worry about spreading myself too thin. They can be happy shagging one another, as well as me.

Assuming they want to keep on shagging me and I haven't screwed things up.

Believe in it, Iris.

I look at Reid. Then Wynter. Then Max.

I want this. It's time to make it happen.

I smack a kiss on Reid's lips, before moving on to crush Max in a hug and kiss him too, then to Wynter. He cocks a brow. "Yes, flirt?"

"You want one of those, too?"

For a heartbeat, I'm afraid he'll say no.

"Yeah, Iris. Yeah, I do."

He opens his arms, and I throw myself into his embrace.

"Fuck!" I hear Reid gripe. I pull away from

Wynter, enough to turn my head, though he keeps on kissing my throat, and making me all jelly-limbed. "The cruel prince strikes again."

"What's that?" I ask.

"Wynter always gets the girl in the end," Max says returning to the fireside. He bends and sets about lighting it. "It's just the way it is." He strikes a match and applies it to the kindling.

"Oh," I say, and back up a little. Wynter just follows.

"It's okay, Iris. We get it. He's hot. And he's new and exciting," Max continues.

"Wait.... No. I mean..." I look to him and then across to Reid. "This isn't me choosing him over you, either of you.

"Maybe we should sit down and talk." Max herds us all towards the sofa, which is still not big enough for all of us. I wind up perched on the arm with my feet in Max's lap, while Wynter and Reid occupy the other end.

"It'd be cool if we could negotiate this sensibly," Max says.

Wynter and Reid look up keenly, and then all three men look at me.

"What exactly are we negotiating?"

"Now and tomorrow," Wynter says. "Iris, do you want to be in a relationship with us?"

I suck my lips together. Tears prickle my eyes. I do. I so desperately want this. It's still hard to let that desire out into the world and not keep it tucked inside my chest, all safe and tiny, rather than setting it free and allowing it to grow into something sprawling and messy and likely painful too. I goldfish my mouth a few times, but the requisite 'yes' fails to come out.

"Argh! Everybody be fucking honest, okay? On a scale of one to ten how much do you want to get laid tonight? Show of fingers, now." Reid signals ten before he even stops talking.

After a moment, Max does the same, as does Wynter.

"Iris?" the latter prompts. "It's a straightforward question."

I uncurl my fingers. Why is this easier than saying yes?

"That's pretty unanimous," Max says, pushing his sleeves up.

"All we've established is that everyone is horny," Wynter contributes.

"Question two. Iris—"

"Don't just pick on me."

"Fine. Stick your mitts up if you're cool with the idea of us all getting it on together." There's another tentative show of hands.

"And hands up again if you want this to be an ongoing affair."

To everyone's astonishment Wynter puts his hand up first. "What?" The incline in his ski-slope brows increases. "You said we had to be fucking honest, so I'm being fucking honest. If it works and we're happy with it, then why not pursue it?"

"No arguments from me," Reid says.

"Max?"

"As long as there's not a rule that says we've always all got to be together. I like alone cuddle time with Iris."

"Any of us can pair up, or throuple up, any way we like. If you're fine with that, say, yay."

They all say yay.

"Iris?"

It's big girl panties time. "Yay." My voice comes out so high-pitched it makes everyone laugh. When they stop, I remove my fingers from in front of my mouth and look to each of them in turn. They're all so different, but that's what makes this perfect. Each of them offers something the others don't. Max with his hugs. Impish Reid, and Wynter, the man I'm only just starting to get to know. "I want tonight, and tomorrow," I say, my voice finding its strength. "I'd like a lot of tomorrows. A lot of tomorrows with all of you, and I hope you want the same with me."

"Fucking course we do." Reid tips forward onto his knees. "Max, some party hats, please, we need to celebrate. Ariel, get your beautiful arse down here, honey." He pats the sofa.

Max gets up, and I slide off the arm into the space he's just vacated. Reid leans over my lap and slides a hand along my jaw and into my hair. I meet his warm hazel eyes and my heart throbs an extra beat. Our mouths meet in a slow collision, while Max and Wynter close in on either side of me. They touch me, stroking my neck, my shoulders, and thighs, then Max cups one breast and Wynter the other. I lose my borrowed shirt and jeans. Max undoes his fly. I put my hands on him, while Reid continues to destroy me with his kisses. He and Wynter swap places, so that Reid is knelt beside me on the sofa, and Wynter's between my legs.

I guess it makes sense that we'd cement our relationship all together like this.

Wynter kisses my inner thighs, while his hand slides up the right. It's my first time with him. It makes me a little shy, or as shy as you can be when three men are undressing and caressing you.

I'm relieved of my panties and am thus left naked between the three still clothed men. Reid immediately ditches his T-shirt, presenting me with his now familiar inked chest.

Wynter's mouth looms over my split. "Please," I gasp.

He pauses. Sheds his shirt while my eyes rake him in hungered arousal. Fuck, he's pretty. Honed to wiry perfection. Not a speck of hair on him, his nipples pastel pink spokes.

"Where is it you want to feel my mouth, Iris?"

As if he doesn't know. I find my clit with my index finger and circle around it.

"There? Right there?"

I nod.

"Exactly here?" He mimics my movement, only with his tongue. Hell yeah, he's got it. I cry out. A cry that Reid swallows. This whole situation has me excited in a way that I can't fully wrap my head around.

I'm fucking all three members of Lucidity. Three men I just agreed to be in a relationship with, and who agreed to be in one with me. This is surreal.

Wynter continues to nuzzle his face between my legs. He stays there until Reid slithers onto the floor beside him. He wraps a hand around the back of his friend's neck and draws him to him. They kiss open-mouthed, completely uninhibited.

Oh, to have my camera on me right now.

But it's okay to sit back and enjoy, it's okay, because there'll be more moments, so many more moments.

Reid winks at me when they part. They take turns beneath my thighs, for a while. Eventually, Reid turns his attention to Wynter, unbuttons him, and tugs down both his jeans and his briefs baring his arse and his cock. I barely get to see it, before Reid starts enthusiastically blowing him.

"That get you humming?" Max says into my ear. He teases the lobe, explores lower, finding every nerve ending in my throat, while he plays with my breasts.

Mouth opening around constant gasps, I watch Wynter's back arch, his head tilt back. His mouth is wide open too. I know how attuned Reid is when he's licking my pussy; he shows the same commitment to getting his boyfriend off.

Wynter presses a hand to the back of his throat. "I don't want to come yet," he says, while looking at me. Reid raises his head. Sees that look.

"Ah, of course, you've not had the pleasure yet. Pass a johnny, Max, our friend here needs one."

I've never seen a man roll a condom down another man's shaft. There's something crazy intimate about it. More intimate than what I've already witnessed.

"You wanting some of this?" I ask Wynter, parting my pussy lips with the splayed fingers of one hand.

He grabs my legs, tugs me to the very edge of the sofa, and rubs his crown in the pool of heat at the juncture of my thighs. "Say you want it, Iris."

"I want it."

"Say you need it."

"I need it. I need you. Show me what you can do."

He fills me in one stroke. He doesn't fuck like either Reid or Max. They're all different. All unique in the way they fill me. Wynter wedges a hand between us and churns his thumb against my clit as he grinds our bodies together. It sets off sparklers and paints heat across my body. I reach out to drag him closer, so that I can seal our lips, but he resists my efforts, goes as far as getting Reid to hold my hands captive.

It's like he's determined to have his way, to keep a little of himself from me. I wriggle my way out of Reid's hold and claw at his body instead, something he certainly doesn't object to.

I lick. I suck. We rub up against one another. This is the best sex I've ever had. How lucky am I that I get to experience it with the three men I've worshipped from afar, and over the course of last week I've come to love.

"Eyes on me, Iris," Wynter demands.

I'd still like to get my hands all over him.

"You listening? I need you to come for me. I want to feel those muscles fluttering around me. You get me?"

Wynter. He's so bossy.

I kinda like it. Plus, I'm close, after such sustained attention. Still not going to magically come on demand, mind. I mutter words to that effect, probably not very coherent ones, given that arousal has made my voice slurry.

Amusement shoots straight into Wynter's eyes, igniting the green. "Yeah, but Ariel, when I say let go? You're going to let go."

"You're not a mesmerist."

"You sure about that?"

I'm not sure about anything anymore, at least not enough to bet my life savings on.

He presses his thumb on my clit, knuckles curled against my abdomen. I don't understand it, but it's like he's squeezing something inside of me, and I can't get enough of it. I skate closer to release. My nipples are now two flushed peaks. He bites. He fucking leaves teeth-marks behind.

"So close." His thrusts slow. He does something that changes the angle of him inside of me. "And...now." He sends me over the edge, like it's no effort at all.

I let the flood of it consume me. I succumb. Ride that wave of rapture. Wynter pulls out of me and peels off the condom. He finishes over my belly. I'm startled by how intimate that makes it feel.

Messy, too, mind.

Right on cue, Reid's there on clean-up duty. He licks me until every drop is gone.

It's only once he's done that I realise Max has completely undressed and is sitting on the sofa jacking himself off.

"Want some of that next?" Reid whispers in my ear. "Now that Wynter's warmed you up?"

God, yes, I want it, even though it makes me feel greedy.

Fuck that.

It's pleasure we all deserve.

Wynter and Reid lift me between them and settle me on Max's lap with my back to his torso. I'm about to protest. I want to be face-to-face with my gentle giant, but then I think about what I might miss if Reid and Wynter are out of my field of view.

"Lift, Iris."

Max wraps his cock and then positions himself. He pushes up as I sink down. I encompass less than half of him at first. It takes some jostling, and riding him at a steady pace before I can take him to the root. He's a big guy, and proportionally big all over. When I do take him all the way, it leaves me splayed wide.

Reid uses that as an invitation to go down. His tongue finds my clit but barely lingers. Rather, his attention roams, taking him to the juncture of my and Max's genitals. He licks me. He licks his bandmates shaft.

"Fucker," Max groans and croons, rocking into me harder. "Suck 'em. Yeah!"

Reid sucks Max's balls, and I suspect even gives his pucker a tickle. Max comes urgently as a result, flooding the condom with his release.

Reid topples backward with a self-satisfied grin on his face. "My turn." He stretches out on his back, kicks off his joggers and rolls on a condom, then beckons me with a curl of his finger. "Come and get it, Ariel. You know you want to."

It happens that he's right. My inhibitions have flown, along with my reservations. There's even something deliciously subversive about sinking over him while I'm still wet from having two other men fuck me.

He makes another few deep strokes, getting us familiar.

It's not long before he gets a glazed sort of look in his eyes.

"Don't come yet." He sighs, mouth open. "Need this to last a little bit more. Fuck, you feel so fucking good. You're absolutely sopping. I love it. I love you. I fucking love you."

"I love you, too."

I feel breath on my neck, and a hand brushes my hair aside. Wynter presses against my back. "You don't mind if I intrude on this love fest, do you?" He begins grinding against me in a way that pushes his cock against my arse. He's at full tilt again. Fast recovery time.

"Is this virgin territory?" he asks, massaging his cock against my pucker. He begins grinding against me, more insistently. Reid's thrusts push me against him, again and again, so that his cock slides into my crack and nudges my hole. "I'm kinda hoping not, much as I'd enjoy being your first—"

"It's not."

"So, you're game?"

Max, who I suspect might have drifted off for a moment after his O, jerks upright. "Man, I love it when you two do it together."

Together!

"What do you think, Iris?"

"She's game. You're game, right?" Reid grasps my hand and kisses my knuckles. "You'll love it. That's a promise."

Lube appears. I've no idea from where. I'm grateful, nevertheless. Wynter gets both himself and my arse slippery. He strokes around the rim, coaxing my muscles to relax and let him in. It feels strange, and I'm all nerves again.

"Jeez, hurry it up, man," Reid encourages, the muscles of his abs jumping as he attempts to hold himself in check. It's clear he's desperate to move. I, too, want him to move. "I'm literally dying here, dude."

"Well then, tell her to relax her arse more."

"Please, Ariel."

"I am relaxed," I say. If I get any more relaxed, I'll be limp. "I just don't regularly let guys fuck my arse." He has at least two whole fingers inside me now.

"That's about to change, honey. You signed up for keeping three horny blokes satisfied. Reid, a little help here."

Reid lifts his head and targets my nipples, proving to be the distraction I need. I stop focusing so hard on what's going on behind me and let myself experience the sensations of Wynter's fingers stretching me and the buzz like connection that ignites between my nipples, my pussy, and my arse.

"I'm gonna fuck your arse real good, Little Mermaid." Wynter removes his fingers from me, and then I feel his crown pressing determinedly.

My muscles protest, but then my body adapts, and it feels amazing.

"Deeper, get in deeper. You know I'm into it when I can feel you rubbing against me." Reid ploughs me as deep as he can. I wonder how I never saw it before meeting them, this bond that exists between Reid and Wynter. This isn't a first for them, even if it is for me. I'm a little jealous of whoever's come before. Then again, I'm also pleased to be benefitting from the practice sessions they offered my men.

Wynter withdraws, then sinks back in pushing deeper. It brings a rush of blood to my face, and a fresh flood of arousal to my pussy. Both men hiss when they feel one another lodged side by side with only a thin barrier between them.

"I fucking live for this," Reid announces. His teeth are bared. There's a feral gleam in his eyes. "You're the best, Ariel. Mermaids for the win."

There is something special about the three of us being connected this way. It's tight, and a bit awkward, but it makes everything sensation-heavy. Consequently, I'm too far gone to understand what's happening when the weight behind me alters. Wynter stiffens and grunts. His whole body flushes hot against my back.

"Fucking, yeah," Reid mouths. "Do him, man."

Wynter's head dips to my shoulder and he curses into my skin. While his bites muffle the sound, it doesn't lessen the way he's quaking. He jerks into me, faster, desperate. He's on the verge. We all are. Me. Wynter. Reid, beneath me. Max... I hear Max, right before I catch a glimpse of him reflected in Reid's blown-wide pupils. Max on his knees behind Wynter.

No, not just behind him. Closer than that. He's inside him.

Now I understand. All four of us are fucking together.

My mind melts. I'm caught by the idea, ravished by it, and driven into raptures. Reid comes in time with the first contraction of my pussy around his shaft. Wynter holds it together for not much longer. He comes so hard that the rush steals his voice. As for me, I'm not sure where my orgasm ends and where it simply collides with theirs. With everything pulsing at once, the lines are blurry.

17

Iris

RIC LIDDELL ANSWERS his door wearing a pair of leather jeans, with his fly at half-mast and something that I suspect may be strawberry sauce smeared across his chest. "Hey," he says.

I only mean to return the camera, not step inside, but he doesn't take it when I hold it out. Instead, he about turns leaving me to follow. In his studio, there's a man handcuffed to an overhead beam, turned away from me in a puddle of the very same sauce.

He waves a hand towards the figure. "This is my husband, Zach Blackwater. Zach, Iris, the fool who asked me about an apprenticeship."

His ridiculously sculpted, very naked husband turns his head and gives me a nod, whereupon I realise that not only is he bound and gagged, he's painfully erect. I'm not sure if I've interrupted a shoot, a make-out session, or a combination of the two.

"Zach owns Blackwater's."

"The food was amazing." Eep, awkward! "We were there the other night."

It's interesting how much Zach manages to convey with just his facial expressions. Evidently, he's aware of Reid's accident with the candle. He probably wasn't too thrilled to have his oysters languishing on the floor either.

"Lucidity are leaving today, right?" Ric drags my attention back to him.

"That's right. I brought you back your camera."

"With something to look at on it for me?"

I'd hoped to be far away before he judged my efforts. Instead, I'm forced to stand as he flicks through a week's worth of images. It's a toss-up as to whether Zach or I find this more excruciating. He's naked, gagged and chained in front of a stranger, and my innards are knotting themselves so tight I might need surgery to untie them again.

"There's some nice shots of Reid. I like this one of Wynter. Is this the direction you're thinking of pursuing—rock photography?"

"I'd like to—"

He's connected the camera to his computer, projecting the images onto the wall. He skims past most of them but flicks back and forth between five or six grainy, black-and-white images of the guys in the studio, eventually honing in on one of Reid playing, in which Wynter's reflection appears to be standing next to him. It's the look on Wynter's face that makes it interesting, not merely the effect.

Ric sucks on the edge of his lower lip.

He flicks through some more of the week. Pauses a few times. Eventually, he goes back to the studio photo. "It's got good texture. It certainly captures a moment. Yeah, okay."

Yeah, okay, what?

He hands me the camera back. "Keep it."

It's the sort of camera I'd have to take a loan out to own.

"You don't own anything this good, right?"

I'm so stunned; it takes all my effort just to shake my head.

"I want to see more of this." He nods at the wall. "If you go on the road with them, you stick like fucking glue to them. Be a fly on the wall. Give us all the moments that we'd never normally see. Show us the underbelly, the warts, the dark. Give us intimacy. Do you think you can do that, Iris?"

"I... I can try."

"The correct response is, yes, sir."

"Yes, sir," I say. How can a man wearing strawberry sauce be so intimidating?

He nods his approval. "I can't be arsed to fuck about with bank details at the moment." He produces a chequebook, and a goddamned fountain pen. "Iris Allen, correct?"

"Yes." He tears the slip from the book and waves it in the air to dry the ink, then puts it in my hand. "I'm investing in you. I'm expecting to see some output that justifies that."

I look at the figure and nearly wet myself.

"That's your cue to exit. Zach has human limits, even if he's superhumanly sexy."

18

IRIS

I STOW THE cheque in my back pocket, where I'm sure it's going to self-ignite.

There are another four cars in the restaurant's shore side carpark in addition to those there earlier. The squeals of children reach me from further along the shore, where the publicly accessible beach lies. They mingle with the screeching of the gulls overhead.

There's no sign of the boys yet. I rest against the side of Wynter's Merc.

A car door opens to my rear. I hear the crunch of shifting gravel. A shadow slides over my feet as a figure blocks out the sun. I turn my head, and he's there. *Harrison* is there.

He's here.

A chill penetrates my skin. Harrison makes a grab for me and catches a handful of hair, wrenches on it so hard that it snaps my head back and makes me screech from the pain.

"Think you're clever, don'tcha. Taking a leap. Not coming home. Here's the thing, Iris, honey. If you don't want to be found, you might want to avoid having your picture taken with celebrities."

I didn't.

"Didn't require any genius to work out where you were holed up after your face got splashed around on social media, and the ever-helpful public pointed out that yeah, that missing local lass isn't really missing at all. She's just off being a slut for her favourite fucking rock band."

The women, that night at Blackwater's. They must have taken pictures of me with the guys.

I twist, attempting to free myself, even at the expense of my hair.

"It's time to come home, Iris. Mum's been distraught. You're going to be a good girl, now, and make her happy. You owe her, after the grief you've caused her."

"I'm not going anywhere with you. You fucking arsehole. Let go." I kick at his legs, twisting and clawing at his arms. "You're a fucking psycho."

"And you're a dirty bitch. How many pricks have you sucked this last week to make sure you had a bed? They ain't kept you around for your intellect. I'm gonna have to bleach your fucking mouth."

He starts dragging me away from the car. My feet slide. It's impossible to maintain any stance on the shifting gravel. I realise he's pulling me towards the end vehicle, the engine of which is running. His friend Lewis sits behind the wheel, baseball cap pulled low over his brow.

No.

I aim a kick and connect with the back of his leg. It buckles. I lash out at his face when he twists to snarl at me. My nails score his cheek, leaving behind four fat, scarlet stripes. His grip releases. I duck, and his hand sweeps ineffectually over my head. I hop backwards, turn, lurch into a sprint.

I'm not going back. I'm never going back. It took me a while, but I've chosen my future and no one, especially not Harrison, is taking that away from me.

Free.

I run for the restaurant. It's closed at this time of day, but beyond it lies the path towards the studio. The shingle makes each step agony. My feet sink to my ankles.

He's going to catch me.

I can't let him catch me.

I'm running, and the past and present collide in my mind. It's now. It's a week ago. It's day. It's night. Harrison is at my heels.

I reach the restaurant. My legs are jelly. I regret every minute of strenuous activity I've engaged in these last few days. I don't have enough power left. My face is wet. I realise I'm crying. The tears blind me.

I need a weapon.

The chairs are too heavy. There must be something.

Candelabra.

I feel his presence. His hands snatch at the back of my shirt, making my skin crawl as if I've ants swarming over me. In frustration, I swing, grunting like a tennis player when the metal connects with his flesh. I hit with everything I've damn well got.

Three figures sweep in from the sides, like something from a movie.

I'm no longer alone. Now it's four against one. Odds I like a whole lot better. The shock on Harrison's face, right before he hits the deck, is pure comedy. Blood splatters the shingle. Max drags Harrison to his feet again.

Reid's not done.

"How dare you lay a fucking hand on her?" He boxes. It's evident in his foot work, in the guard, in the power of his fist as it connects. It explains that physique I've explored and admired so much. He whips Harrison with an upper cut then knees him in the face as he folds.

Thai boxer?

Max kicks him in the arse, which shunts Harrison forward so that he lands on his face.

Wynter lifts him by the hair. "I'm going to count to five. At the end of it, you'd better pray you're halfway across that fucking causeway, or I'm going to feed you to the fucking fishes. One..."

Harrison stumbles on unsteady legs, a hand clasped to his now bleeding nose. There's salt in the air, that isn't purely the sea. There's no way he'll reach the causeway in time, but I realise that's the point. Wynter's just looking for an excuse.

Lewis throws his car into reverse, creating a spray of sand and stones. He meets Harrison, throwing the passenger door open for him to dive inside. He slams the car door, right as Wynter hits five.

No one gives chase.

There's no need. Lewis floors it toward the causeway, massively exceeding the speed limit. If they wind up in the water, I won't mourn.

"Good fucking riddance, you fucking arsehole." I'm possible still a teeny bit irate, and my head is sore.

Reid gently teases my hand open and returns the candelabra to the table. "Big guy," he prompts, even as I'm already turning to Max for a hug. I bury my face in his pec, snuffling.

"I've got ya. It's going to be fine. You're okay, Iris."

Wynter retrieves the camera from by the car where I must have dropped it. I don't even recall doing so. Thankfully, it's undamaged, bar a little bit of dust that's easily brushed off. "Haven't you seen Ric yet?"

"I get to keep it." I gasp around the thickness and panic that still resides in my throat. The drama is over now, and I'm safe. Max still has me in a protective swaddle. "Ric's giving me a chance."

"What sort of chance?"

I show them the cheque.

"Well fuck me!" Reid whoops. "You fucking nailed it. Did I not tell you; you had this in the bag?"

He did.

"It was all those yummy pictures of me, right?"

It wasn't, but he doesn't need to know that. It was a shot of Wynter that swayed it. One image that made Ric pause for long enough that he was prepared to consider nurturing the talent that captured it. Now, all I have to do is make that potential bear fruit.

Wynter whistles over the number of zeros on the cheque. "What's the plan, Iris? How are you—"

"Nothing's changed. You're still stuck with me," I say, cutting him off because I'm not going to waste my time living up to anyone's expectations. Which isn't to say I don't want to impress Ric, I do, but I want to enjoy the opportunity I've been given, too. "Shall we go, guys?"

We cross the causeway back to the mainland, and I grin the whole way.

Six months later.

SPOTLIGHTS SWEEP ABOVE the heads of the gathered festival goers. I'm at the side of the stage on which Lucidity are about to perform. It's dark. The crowd stretches into the distance. The only lights are those that illuminate the stage.

"Good evening, Equinox."

The spotlights coalesce on Wynter, bass slung low.

There's a rumble of voices as the crowd respond.

"We're Lucidity. This is the title track from our new album, which drops at midnight."

The crowd roar.

Wynter leans in closer to the microphone. Max's drums kick in, followed by that now familiar riff.

"This is *Weep*, and it's dedicated to a very

special friend. You'll find her gorgeous photography on the album sleeve."

ABOUT THE AUTHOR

MADELYNNE IS A New York Times & USA Today bestselling author. She wrote her first novel after discovering Black Lace Books in the 1990s. After escaping the Hotel California, she dived into storytelling full time. Her books are filled with bisexual bad boys who like to get down and dirty, and stories so angst-filled you know they're going to hurt.

She lives in the UK near the Welsh border, where you can find her surrounded by books, drinking rapidly cooling decaf coffee, and listening to loud music.

Come hang out with her via her newsletter, where she shares what she's reading, watching, listening to, and snippets about her current projects.